Windfall and Other Stories

SOUTHWEST LIFE AND LETTERS

A series designed to publish outstanding new fiction and nonfiction about Texas and the American Southwest and to present classic works of the region in handsome new editions.

General Editors: Suzanne Comer, Southern Methodist University Press; Tom Pilkington, Tarleton State University.

WINDFALL

and Other Stories

Winifred M. Sanford

Foreword by Emerett Sanford Miles

Afterword by Lou Halsell Rodenberger

SOUTHERN METHODIST UNIVERSITY PRESS

First Southern Methodist University Press edition, 1988
Requests for permission to reproduce material from this work should be sent to:
    Permissions
    Southern Methodist University Press
    Box 415
    Dallas, Texas 75275

Library of Congress Cataloging-in-Publication Data

Sanford, Winifred M., 1890–
    Windfall and other stories.

    (Southwest life and letters)
    1. Texas—Fiction. I. Title. II. Series:
Southwest life & letters.
PS3537.A696W5   1988   813′.52   87-43105
ISBN 0-87074-267-1
ISBN 0-87074-268-X (pbk.)

Design by Whitehead & Whitehead

COVER ART: "Oil Field Girls" by Jerry Bywaters. Courtesy
Archer M. Huntington Art Gallery, The University of Texas at Austin,
Michener Collection Acquisition Fund, 1984.

Contents

Winifred M. Sanford

Foreword

She was born Winifred Balch Mahon March 16, 1890, in Duluth, Minnesota. Her parents were both from Michigan: the former Nellie Brooks, whose father was a professor of Latin and Greek in Kalamazoo, and Irish-born Henry Mahon, an attorney, from Ann Arbor.

The pictures of her that survive, posed with her cousins at the summer home in Charlevoix, with her graduation class at Duluth Central High School, wearing her young Navy husband's pea jacket as she stands, laughing, on a windy beach, show her to have been something of a beauty. At fourteen she was pretty enough to have had a duel fought for her favors by two schoolmates, one of whom, a gallant youth named Wayland Hall Sanford, was eventually to become her husband. Wayland was proud of his role in the affair and years later showed his children a keepsake, the yellowed handwritten note from his opponent of the day.

> Duluth, Minn.
> Feb. 25, 1904
>
> Mr. W. H. Sanford
>   Dear Sir, I am most pleased to except [*sic*] your challenge. We will duel with boxing gloves at 4:30 P.M. Friday in Mr. P. A. Poirier's shack. Hoping to see you at an early hour,
>   I remain,
>   Your humble servant
>   Max A. Pulford.

She attended Mount Holyoke College in Massachusetts. Later she would recall how much like an outsider she had felt at first. After all, she was not from New England, and Minnesota, particularly Duluth—well, that was the iron ore range. Her classmates were surprised, she said, that she had proper, even fashionable, clothes. And she had been able to buy them right there in Duluth! Later she transferred to the University of Michigan, where she majored in English and made Phi Beta Kappa. She graduated in 1913 and taught school for four years, first in Sault Ste. Marie, Michigan, and then in Idaho (where she remembered her classes as made up entirely of hulking boys twice her size). By 1916 she had tired of teaching. She moved to New York City, where she lived with her mother. Wayland was in law school then, at the University of Michigan. In 1917 he graduated, entered the Navy, and he and Winifred began to make wedding plans.

A favorite family story, which she herself loved to tell, concerned an event that took place during this period. Wayland, an officer candidate at Annapolis, received an unexpected pass. They had been waiting for just such an opportunity to be married but, unfortunately, she was already on her way to spend the weekend on Long Island with a friend who had no telephone. Hoping there was still time to stop her at the railroad station, Wayland called Grand Central to have her paged. Winifred would laugh a little ruefully as she got to this point in the story, trying to explain how it was that as she passed through the ticket line and heard the voice booming over the loudspeaker, "Miss Winifred Mahon, calling Miss Winifred Mahon," she thought to herself: Imagine that! Someone else has a name the same as mine!

Perhaps even then she was preoccupied with working out plot lines, getting acquainted with the characters who would in a few years spring to life in the pages of *The American Mercury* and *Woman's Home Companion*. In any event, they were married some weeks later at the Little Church around the Corner in New York City.

When the war ended Winifred settled temporarily in Duluth

waiting the birth of their first child while Wayland scouted rumors of a new oil strike in Texas where a young attorney interested in the practice of oil and gas law might find a demand for his services. The baby was eight months old when Winifred joined him in Wichita Falls, near the booming Burkburnett oil field in North Texas. There, a year later, a second daughter was born.

In Texas she saw her first oil derricks. She met geologists, engineers, roughnecks and drillers, speculators, promoters, swindlers, and dreamers—all the rich variety of people drawn to gold rushes, oil booms, and other treasure hunts. In Wichita Falls she found a fertile source of characters and plots. In addition to the outsiders who, like Winifred and Wayland themselves, had been attracted by the boom, there were the country folk on whose land the derricks stood, and the townspeople whose lives also had been changed, for better or worse, by the discovery of oil. Years later, after she had moved to Dallas, she still marveled at the great diversity she had found in Wichita Falls, and she missed it.

Some of her finest short stories concerned these people of the oil fields. She told her stories from the fringes of the oil business through the eyes of ordinary people caught up in it, not the millionaires, whom she also knew, or the "company" people, or the lawyers.

In Wichita Falls, too, she attended her first revival meeting and out of that experience wrote "Saved." She took her two young daughters with her and they still remember something of the fearful emotion evoked in the great tent by the voice of the evangelist, the impassioned hymn-singing, so different from the staid Episcopal Church to which they were accustomed, and the sawdust on the floor that made them cough.

Her first published stories, however, were set in the Lake Superior country she had known so well. By the time the first, "Wreck," was written she had polished her technique and craftsmanship through long practice. About this story, she wrote in a letter to William R. Kane, editor of *The Editor Magazine*, early in 1926:

I remember every step of its development because it marked the beginning of what was for me a new point of view and a new style —the ironic! . . . I started out to overwhelm the reader with the tragedy of it by direct methods . . . I made two separate attempts to do it before I had the idea I later developed, to tell it indirectly through two good-for-nothing characters who were almost entirely insensible of the tragedy they were witnessing. . . .

H. L. Mencken bought "Wreck" for *The American Mercury*, and as long as he was editor he continued to encourage her. A typical note from him begins:

Have you anything in hand or in mind that would fit into *The American Mercury?* It seems a long, long while since I last heard from you.

She was torn, in those years, between her need to write and her duties as a wife and mother. There were two daughters now, Emerett and Helen. She had little time of her own. In 1927 she wrote to David Lloyd, of Paget Literary Agency, who had approached her about representing her:

I have been writing only a few years, and since I am married and have small children, I have so far been unable to give full professional time to my typewriter. . . .

Mencken was constantly exhorting her to send more material. *Woman's Home Companion* was a ready market. Such honors as being named in E. J. O'Brien's *Best Short Stories* of 1926 came her way. A college textbook used a passage from "The Blue Spruce" as a model; another reprinted "Windfall." M. K. Singleton, in his 1962 book *H. L. Mencken and the "American Mercury" Adventure*, called her stories "among the best in the *Mercury*." What she did was very good and, according to another letter to David Lloyd, she sold everything she wrote, "except for a few practice stories in the beginning."

Yet there were, in all, only thirteen stories, published over a period of seven years.

She was tempted early on to abandon the short story form for novels. In a letter dated February 6, 1926, she wrote to Gertrude B. Lane, editor of *Woman's Home Companion*:

> I have been working day and night, almost, on a novel, and except for three or four short stories written for *The American Mercury* at Mr. Mencken's solicitation, I have done nothing else.

In late 1927 she mentioned to David Lloyd that she had sent the novel directly to Knopf, which had rejected it with the option to "reconsider it later." The book, tentatively called *Arrows of the Almighty*, did not sell, after all, although most of the major publishing houses expressed genuine interest, and even regret, at turning it down. As late as 1932 her agent was writing for "news of the novel," which she was evidently revising, but nothing ever came of it and she finally reduced the manuscript to ashes in the family fireplace. At one point, Mencken wrote:

> It is excellent news that you are full of doubts about your novel. The bad ones are all written by authors who are absolutely sure of them!

This letter, as were most of his, was undated. He continued to encourage her, particularly when she reacted to criticism. He admonished her:

> Everyone I know thought "Wreck" was excellent stuff. And it undoubtedly was! Don't let imbeciles annoy you.

And later:

> Please pay no heed to such foolish advice. "Black Child" is one of the best stories you have done.

And still later:

Please don't pay any attention to newspaper discussions of your writings. Nine times out of ten they are completely idiotic. I detest all labeling. A good story is a good story. . . . As I wrote you some time ago, Kathleen Norris is a very enthusiastic admirer of your work. . . . She is a very intelligent woman and knows a good story when she sees it.

The *Mercury* published her first story in January 1925. By 1928 Mencken had used six more and three had appeared in *Woman's Home Companion*, the leading women's magazine of the day. Two more in the *Mercury* and a final one in *North American Review*, and by 1931 her writing career was over. In May 1929 she wrote Mencken:

I wish I *did* have something worth printing. I have a dozen things in mind but nothing I have written for the last year has pleased me or anyone else. If I were only sure that the bird would rise from the ashes, I would light a large bonfire.

Whether it was the novel, which occupied so much of her creative time and with which she was so determined to succeed, that drew her away from the craft of short story writing, or the birth of a third daughter, Mary, after the family moved to Dallas, or the lengthy bout with tuberculosis that kept her in bed for two years, she herself did not know. One might speculate, though, that when her husband established his law office in Longview, center of the new East Texas oil boom, and the family moved to Dallas in 1931 to be closer to him, she left behind a great deal of her creative inspiration in Wichita Falls. She missed the colorful people, the activity, the closeness of a smaller town. And she missed, particularly, the fellowship of the other writers and would-be writers whom she had helped organize into a group called the Manuscript Club. In 1945, fourteen years after the move to Dallas, she spoke rather wistfully of the Manuscript Club in a letter to Margaret Cousins, editor of *Good Housekeeping*:

I think you would agree with me that a group of that sort is of much more value to a writer than an outsider would suppose. It is so much more than a mere giving and taking of criticism. The air seems thick with ideas whenever you get together. You are put on your mettle; the old competitive spirit rises in you, and you find yourself writing in spite of yourself. . . .

Perhaps if she had remained in Wichita Falls that "old competitive spirit" would have kept her at her craft. On the other hand, it is more likely that she no longer had the driving need to write.

New interests grew to fill her days, and she went on to other things. Having survived several seemingly catastrophic illnesses in her lifetime, she died at 93, hardly sick at all. She had never feared death, and it would have pleased her that the minister thought it appropriate at her funeral to quote from her story "The Monument": "Oh, but dying takes such a minute, Julia. It's living that takes the time and the courage."

Emerett Sanford Miles

A Chronology of Winifred M. Sanford's Publications

January 1925	"Wreck"	*The American Mercury*
April 1925	"The Forest Fire"	*The American Mercury*
June 1925	"Allie"	*The American Mercury*
January 1926	"Saved"	*The American Mercury*
January 1926	"The Monument"	*Woman's Home Companion*
May 1926	"Mary"	*Woman's Home Companion*
May 1926	"The Blue Spruce"	*The American Mercury*
January 1927	"Black Child"	*The American Mercury*
January 1928	"Fools"	*Woman's Home Companion*
June 1928	"Windfall"	*The American Mercury*

September 1930	"Luck"	*The American Mercury*
April 1931	"Mr. Carmichael's Room"	*The American Mercury*
November 1931	"Fever in the South"	*North American Review*

These stories were collected in the volume *Windfall and Other Stories*, which was privately published by the Sanford family in 1980 and is the basis for the present collection. Included in the family-published volume also were "A Victorian Grandmother" and "Fannie Baker," the latter of which—a "true story of a doll (which is still in the family) written for the author's small daughters"—has been omitted from this volume.

Windfall and Other Stories

Wreck

Elsie didn't see the *Harvey Jones* go on the rocks because she was so mad at Charlie that she didn't care about watching freighters rolling about on the lake, even though Alec McFee, who was the cause of the present trouble, was on board. She was, if anything, rather glad when her sister Mame cried out the news from the front window. She thought it would serve Alec right to get a good scare.

"Elsie, it missed the channel! Come here quick!"

Elsie got out of her rocking chair by the fire with considerable effort—she was plumper than she used to be—and shuffled over to the window in her felt slippers. Mame had rubbed a clear circle out of the frost that encrusted the glass.

"Land's sake!" said Elsie.

She blinked at the *Harvey Jones* and then she giggled. Honestly, she couldn't help it. It was too funny to see that great big freighter lying crosswise in the shallow water, with the waves going over her. Guess it must have surprised them some to be picked up by the sea just when they thought they were safe in the ship canal, and carried clear over the pier, and dumped down on the rocks like a good-for-nothing piece of driftwood.

"Don't that beat all!" said Elsie, feeling cross again. "On Charlie's day off. Two wrecks on Charlie's day off."

It was bad enough, she ruminated, scratching idly at the frost on the window, to have a beau who was on the lifesaving crew, and tied down to hours and days, with a fool like Anderson to tell him

3

what he could do and what he couldn't, without having wrecks to spoil your fun. Everytime they planned anything . . . a wreck or an accident! Last summer a girl had tipped over in a canoe and ruined their picnic. Charlie had spent three dandy moonlit hours dragging with grappling hooks. Nasty business! She had told him a thousand times to quit and take another job. Maybe now that he had had two wrecks in one day, he wouldn't have so much to say about its being an easy life. Just wait till he got back from Stony Point, or wherever it was those fishermen were in trouble, all wet and tired and hungry, and found the *Harvey Jones* pounding on the rocks. Say, wouldn't Charlie be sore! The very last week, too, before navigation closed for the winter.

Mame took her green sweater out of the closet.

"You're crazy," said Elsie. "When you can see everything there is to see from here."

But Mame put it on, and her coat as well, though it was a tight fit. She also found an old cap of her husband's with earflaps, which she fastened with a safety pin under her chin.

"Where's my mittens?"

"I wouldn't go out in the blizzard for a million dollars," said Elsie.

It did, indeed, nearly sweep Mame off her feet. She had to turn her back and make a windbreak of her shoulders in order to breathe. The white vapor she breathed in the cold was like a scarf blowing over her shoulders. With her head down, she edged along, sideways, toward the beach.

II

As Elsie had said, the *Harvey Jones* was in plain sight from the window. It looked like a projection from the pier, a black breakwater, deluged every minute by an enormous swell of brown water. Lordy, those waves were enough to scare anyone stiff! Thirty feet high, maybe forty, and every one washed clear over the *Harvey Jones*.

Alec McFee would get a good shower bath before night. Well, it wasn't any more than he deserved for trying to make trouble between her and Charlie. Alec McFee was no little tin saint himself that he should go about telling tales on her.

Perhaps Alec was one of those men she could just see in the stern. There didn't seem to be any place for them to go. They just stood there by the smokestack, flapping their arms and stamping their feet, and crouching to take the beating of each successive wave. Weren't they stupid not to make a dash for the bow and the pilothouse where the others were evidently keeping warm and dry? Perfect geese.

My goodness, one of them did try it—the one in the bright red mackinaw! Just after one wave broke, he started running, only it was more like staggering and floundering than like running, but he slipped and was sprawling there on the deck when the next wave crashed down on him. For a minute it looked as if he would be washed overboard—the way the yellow water was rolling him around—but he caught hold of the rope at the side and hung on for dear life. Didn't get up to run, either, just hung there and let another wave nearly drown him, until one of the boys ran out and dragged him back to the smokestack and leaned him up against it like a big rag doll. Crash! Down he went on his face under a ton of water. After a while he got up on all fours and stayed like that. All in, probably.

"Gee, but I'm cold," said Elsie. Her toes were actually numb inside the felt slippers. She could feel the sharp cold blowing in around the edges of the window frame and under the door. Boo, but she did hate to be cold! So she dragged a rag rug over to the door, and folded it against the crack at the bottom, and poured a lot of coal from the scuttle into the top of the heater. It sizzled and crackled.

Tra la! She flopped into the rocking chair, pulling a pink shawl that hung over the back around her shoulders, and planting her felt slippers on the nickel-plated footrest, out of the draft.

Elsie yawned. She hadn't slept much because she was so mad at Charlie. He had looked as ugly as a thundercloud when he had said he was coming up tonight. Very likely he intended to tell her all over again what Alec had whispered to him, and for all she knew he might take back that diamond ring. But Elsie was sure he'd never get as far as that. She knew him too well. He wouldn't stay mad if she laughed and teased him a little, without losing her temper, and fixed him good and comfortable by the stove, and—well, any girl knew how to make a man forget what he didn't mean to forget. He'd be teasing for a kiss in half an hour. So Elsie wasn't worrying any, but she was peeved at Charlie for believing it so easily. And now this darn wreck! No telling when Charlie would get off. And even then he'd be tired and snappy and not likely to listen to reason.

What under the sun was that? Sounded like a gun. Gosh. Elsie bounded to the window again, and had to rub a new peek hole in the frost. Oh, it was just the *Harvey Jones* breaking in the middle. It had popped like a gun and scared Elsie nearly to death. Yellow water gushed through the crack, which widened as the stern settled. Well, boys, you'll wish you'd run for it now, thought Elsie.

Lots of people were down on the shore, curious people like Mame who always wanted to stick their noses into other folks' business. They must like to be cold, she said to herself, noticing how the wind bent them all in the same direction, like the trees in the picnic grove behind the house. The ground was a frozen white, the sky a low gray ceiling, frozen too, and the lake was coldest of all: it was mad, a freezing mad, flinging itself around in the rocks as if it had gone clear crazy.

All at once she saw the lifesavers running along in their shiny slickers with a big white lifeboat on its carriage and the funny little gun they used for the lifelines on practice days. One of them, she knew, was Charlie.

Elsie decided that she had better go out after all, although it was a mean shame that she couldn't have Charlie in here by the fire. It would have been nice to sit here in the rocker, with Charlie

6

sprawled on the floor, so that his yellow head rested in her lap. Nice and warm and drowsy . . .

Elsie had a fur coat which she slipped on over her percale house dress, and a little toque made out of her mother's old seal muff—real Alaska seal. The collar of the coat turned up to meet the hat, snugly. And she had a fat, padded muff for her hands. Elsie always had nice things; when she wanted more, she got a job keeping somebody's books. Just now she was taking life easy at Mame's, but when she and Charlie patched things up, well, she might go to work again so that she could have silk underclothes and silver for her wedding.

Elsie pouted while she pulled on her overshoes. Once Charlie had admired the smallness of her ankles. They were small, too, though her legs were chunky enough . . . but she couldn't freeze for the sake of pleasing Charlie. Not in a northeaster like this.

She powdered carefully the very last thing, and broke off a thread that had raveled from the lining of her coat. All rightie, now; out we go.

III

Wow, what a wind! It whipped the snow in her face, snow that stung like grains of sand. Elsie was swept out of her course, this way and that. The cold blew up inside her clothes, under her hat, into the aching space behind her forehead.

And the sight of the *Harvey Jones* didn't make Elsie feel any warmer. Things looked a lot worse as she came close where she could see the dirty yellow ice plastered all over the deckhouses and the spars, or whatever you called them, and hanging down in long, lumpy icicles. For some reason the dark water looked even colder than the ice—and the drenched and glittering deck looked more like the sluiceway of a dam down which the sea was sliding than a floor which could be walked on.

And those men in the stern! Five of them, and sakes alive!

why, that was Alec McFee in the red mackinaw. What do you know about that! And he came as near as that to being drowned right under her eyes. Yes, that was Alec, squatting on all fours in the water. She guessed he wouldn't have much to say when they pulled him in.

And such a noise! The lake was always noisy; Elsie got awfully tired of hearing it swush up and suck back night after night, even in calm weather, but this afternoon it was simply beside itself. You'd think it was out to break the rocks into splinters; it would gather itself up, and hold its breath for a second, and then it would crash down with an awful echoing roar all over the *Harvey Jones*. Not just once in a while, but every minute or less, maybe, as steady as a clock ticking out the time. It never missed a stroke.

Elsie saw Charlie a long way off—recognized him by the width of his back and the forward tilt of his head, although his slicker and hat were like all the other slickers and hats in the group where he stood. "Come on!" called Mame, arm in arm with a neighbor, but Elsie pretended not to hear. She didn't want them interfering. And Charlie saw her—oh yes, Charlie saw her, in spite of the fact that he was busy setting up the gun.

"Hello!" shouted Elsie. She had to get close to make him hear.

"Hello," sullenly, she could see.

"Tough luck," commiserated Elsie.

"My luck's always tough," growled Charlie, but he looked at her, and because she was smiling as if she liked him, he smiled too, a little.

"Gee, but I'm cold," said Elsie.

Charlie took her arm at that, roughly, as she liked him to take it, and pulled her toward the bonfire some men were building on the rocks. "Get yourself warm, kid, and stick around."

So Elsie, smiling to herself, stuck around. Dusk was upon them, but she didn't mind. She liked night better than day anytime, especially in a crowd, with bonfires burning.

8

The lifeline went out with a whizzing sound. Shucks! Anderson had aimed too low. Elsie circled the bonfire to tease Charlie about it. "You're a great bunch of lifesavers, you are!"

"Look out!" One of the men jostled her impatiently. "Stand back, everybody."

Elsie stood back, just a little, in time to see the second line strike fairly on the afterdeck, and the clumsy bearlike figures lunge out feebly before the wave swept it down on the rocks. Charlie stepped up again while it was being pulled back. "See your friend Alec?" His voice was hoarse, and he spat manfully in the snow.

"He's getting his," said Elsie, tossing her head high.

Zip, out went the line, and was caught this time, squarely, and fastened to something or other. For a minute everything looked fine, until the next wave thundered down. Snapped, would you believe it? Borne down and cut on a rock, as like as not. Anyway, gone.

Well, they could shoot another, dozens of them . . . all the lifelines on the Great Lakes . . . just give them time. Elsie couldn't see all that happened because it was growing darker all the while, but she knew that every single one that caught snapped—like that! And each failure was accompanied by a groan from the crowd, all together, like fans at a ball game.

"We've got to wait for the wind to die down," said Anderson, at last, "and for daylight."

Elsie intercepted Charlie as he passed. "I bet Alec McFee's on his knees, taking back some of his lies."

"Lies, eh?" repeated Charlie. But he was forgiving enough to borrow her muff to warm his hands. Elsie jumped at the touch of them, wet and cold as melting ice.

"You poor baby," she cried.

A man in a fur-lined overcoat tapped Charlie on the shoulder, yelling even louder than was necessary. "What's the matter with you fellows? Got your boat, haven't you?"

9

"Say," returned Charlie, "if you want to take a little pleasure trip in that boat, go ahead, don't mind me, but you'd live just about one minute in that sea. Good night!"

Well, it was true enough. Even Elsie could see the jagged points of rock when the undertow sucked the water away. Over by the ship, the currents, meeting as they rushed around the two ends and down in a cataract through the middle, were swirling in two awful circles that would have spun a boat till it stood on end. Elsie laughed.

"Thinks you're a whale, Charlie."

Other men began asking the same question that the man in the fur-lined overcoat had asked. Some of them even wanted to go, and tramped around on the ice-coated rocks looking for a place to launch a boat until they were stopped by Anderson and the ship's owners, who kept insisting they had troubles enough already.

So instead, more bonfires were built to cheer the men, keep their courage up . . . they went around saying that as they dug driftwood out of the snow . . . "Keep the poor chaps' courage up" . . . The red glare made queer pictures on the underside of the waves and on the dripping decks. Spooky, Elsie thought. The five men didn't move about much now, or flap their arms or stamp their feet, just crouched as if they didn't care what happened.

Presently a man girdled with a white life belt opened the door of the pilothouse up in front, and stepped out between waves. Before he had to run back, he yelled something through a megaphone about "Help . . . for God's sake . . . freezing . . ." The people on the shore began to clamor. Elsie saw two women crying.

IV

It was then that Elsie had a real inspiration. Coffee! She trudged through the snow all the way to Mame's house and back again, fighting the wind, to get the big pot they had used on picnics, and Mame's coffee canister, and cups enough for all the lifesavers.

Charlie scooped up snow, and before anybody saw what they were up to, the coffee was boiling. Anderson, who had never liked her, wouldn't take any, but the others were tickled to death. Anderson walked up and down in the edge of the water, with the spray going all over him, and snorted when spoken to.

"Is he going to keep you out all night?" Elsie asked Charlie as she filled his cup for the fourth time.

"Looks that way, though it ain't my idea of a circus."

"I bet you're dead tired, Charlie. Can't you quit long enough to get your breath?"

Charlie looked at her hard. Then he set down his cup in the snow, and led Elsie to one side. Anderson wasn't watching, so they moved farther, and finally scrambled up a snowbank, and ducked down on the far side behind a clump of cedars. No one was there because the cedars cut off the view of the *Harvey Jones*. But it was warm, or almost warm, out of the wind, and as nice as could be . . . quiet, too, even the booming of the waves deadened by snowbank.

Charlie sat in the snow, opened up his slicker, and spread out one side for her to sit on.

"Looka here," he said. "I want you to tell me straight about this story of Alec's. Is it true, or ain't it?"

Elsie hesitated just an instant. Then she laughed, the way you laugh at a good joke on somebody else.

"You great big baby," she cried. "Of course it wasn't true. Everybody but you knew it was a lie . . . jealous old thing, you." She poked her forefinger under Charlie's chin and made him look at her.

Charlie let out his breath, smiled in a silly fashion, and began to kiss her. His arms were so strong he nearly squeezed the wind out of her.

"You've sure got me going, kid," said Charlie. "You're one sweet girl."

While Elsie rubbed his hands inside her muff, they talked about getting married.

"And a job," begged Elsie. "You'll get another job?"

"Sure thing."

Elsie was fooling with his fingers . . . one, two, three, four, five . . . this little pig went to market . . . ouch! No fair tickling. She was thinking about going to work for a month or so, and about the flesh-colored crepe de chine she would buy for her underclothes . . . with just a touch of black hemstitching . . . chiffon hose, the very best . . . and a velvet dress, a midnight blue velvet dress. Charlie gave forth a terrible sigh.

It was totally dark now, except for the flickering reflection of the bonfire. Elsie yawned. She was beginning to feel stiff from sitting so long in the snow.

"Isn't that someone calling you, Charlie?"

"Lord, it's Anderson. Let me go," Charlie said in a panicky voice.

What Anderson wanted, it developed, was pickaxes.

"What for?" demanded Elsie.

Charlie smiled, kind of funny. "To chip the boys out," he explained, watching Elsie to note the effect of his words. "They'll be a row of icebergs by morning."

Elsie stared at him. His face was a grotesque red and black in the light of the bonfire. The shadow of his nose lay wide and sinister on his ruddy cheek. In spite of herself, she began to shiver.

The long, diverging ray of a searchlight swung out suddenly from the dark, wandered jerkily across the soft and heavy sky, stroked the rolling surface of the water, paused on the ice-trimmed pilot-house of the *Harvey Jones* just long enough to catch the beating of arms and the lifting of heads within, and became transfixed, as if with horror, on the sleek and slippery stern of her. Five dark lumps were huddled under the smokestack, shapeless lumps, a horrid, dirty yellow. A shudder ran like an electric current along the shore. The awful crashing descent of a wave washed them out for an instant, then revealed them again, undisturbed. Five bowed heads, five clumsy, crouching bodies glistened under the searchlight. Nothing human about them. They were part of the ship, and the ship was part of the furnishing of the sea, like the rocks which held her. Wave after wave after wave fell upon them.

Elsie was seized with a panic. Her legs seemed on the point of dissolving and letting her warm body down in the snow. "Gosh!" she said. "Charlie!"

He came up suddenly, with two pickaxes in his hand, and she clutched him. Once before, on a Ferris wheel at the fair, Elsie had been scared, and Charlie had laughed at her just as he was laughing now. You couldn't scare Charlie.

"What's the matter?" he shouted jovially. "You wanted me to change jobs, didn't you? Well, what's the matter with the ice business, eh?"

"Ugh," said Elsie, pretending to slap him. "Aren't you horrid?"

The Forest Fire

At ten o'clock Hattie sprinkled down her washing—twenty-eight sheets and quite as many pillowcases and towels. At eleven she blew out the lamp in the lobby of the little hotel, and went to bed, with no more than a glance at the western sky, which was a brilliant orange red, like a diffused and belated sunset. The forest fires were bad again. The man who drove the mail truck had said he could hardly get past Norway.

"I told you there wouldn't be anybody else coming in," said Alvin.

Hattie didn't see much sense in answering that. After all, there hadn't been anybody else coming in.

At a quarter to twelve she heard a great rumpus overhead. She put on her red eiderdown wrapper and her slippers, lighted a lamp, and climbed the narrow stairs to the second floor of the hotel. For as much as three minutes she stood by the door of No. 202, bending her head to listen. Then she stuffed her pigtails inside the collar of her wrapper, fastened the frayed frogs, and knocked.

A man's voice bawled, "Come in!"

Hattie knocked again.

Presently she heard the key turn, and saw the door open, just a little. Around the edge of it she saw a tangle of rough hair, a bloodshot eye, and a hanging lip. Behind she saw—could not help but see—a thick arm waving a bottle, a glass lying on its side, a jumble of bedclothes.

15

Someone coughed.

"Gentlemen," said Hattie, "I can't have such goings-on in my place. If you've got to make a saloon out of a decent hotel, you've got to do it in quiet. There's folks sleeping all around you, and they've got rights, and so have I. I'm sorry to have to speak to you, gentlemen."

One of the men made a noise like a cat.

"Shut up," mumbled the man at the door.

"Thank you, Mr. Stiegler," said Hattie. "That's all. Good night."

Hattie went back to bed.

"What's the row?" asked Alvin.

"Stiegler again," said Hattie.

She fell asleep at once, and lay like a log until a car stopped under her window. In a minute she heard the burr burr burr of the bell screwed on the front door. She put on her wrapper and her slippers, lighted her lamp, and padded across the dining room and the parlor and the lobby. Through the door, when she opened it, came the soft grating sound of the water on the beach.

"Is this the Griggs Hotel?"

"Yes; what do you want?"

They slid in past her—a young girl, with very short yellow hair curled up tight all over her head, wrapped in a cape of scarlet, and a boy scarcely old enough to vote with a mustache like a shadow and long thin legs.

"Gee, but I'm cold," cried the girl.

"What do you want?" asked Hattie again. She had not yet closed the door.

"What do we want? A place to sleep, thank you."

"And could you give us something to eat?" begged the girl. She was appealing, holding out such white hands.

"Where'd you come from?"

"Yeah," said the boy. "Give us a cup of coffee and some sand-

16

wiches . . . anything you happen to have. We've been driving since seven this morning."

"I asked you where'd you come from?" said Hattie.

The boy bit his lip.

"Say," he stammered, like a really small boy. "It's all right, you know. We live in Minneapolis; we're on our wedding trip."

"Oh," said the girl. She stretched out her left hand, holding it close to the lamp so that Hattie could see the narrow platinum wedding ring fitting so snugly against its jeweled mate. Hattie saw her blue veins under the skin, and the polished nails.

Hattie shut the door and took a key from the rack behind the desk.

"I beg your pardon," she said. "I've got into trouble once or twice. I have to be careful."

They followed her very quietly up the stairs and down the hall to No. 209, where Hattie unlocked the door and lighted the lamp on the commode.

"I'll get you something to eat." She started to go out, paused with the doorknob in her hand, and said, "Minneapolis was my home . . . ," but they didn't hear her.

Hattie boiled coffee on the oil burner kept for such emergencies, made a plateful of sandwiches, and sat down at one of the empty tables while they ate.

"How about this forest fire?" asked the boy.

"I've lived here for fourteen years," said Hattie, "and every fall but three it's been like this."

"Any danger of its coming this way?" The girl stood up to peer through the window, shutting out the lamplight with her hands.

"You can't tell about forest fires," said Hattie. "It all depends on the wind."

They finished presently, and went upstairs. Hattie saw the boy's arm reach around the girl's waist, and she saw the girl turn her face to him.

"Somebody come?" asked Alvin, when she got back to bed.
"Yes."

II

The alarm went off at five, or started to, but Hattie sat up in time to check it. She dressed quietly, washed without splashing, combed her hair, and shut the bedroom door cautiously. Alvin was still asleep.

When she went into the kitchen the dog got up, with his usual senile struggles, and barked to go out. Hattie stood for a moment at the back door. No sky was visible. The spiked tops of the pines were blurred against a cloud of orange smoke. Hattie stepped out into the clearing behind the kitchen and split a pile of kindling with Alvin's axe. With the aid of a dash of kerosene she started the fire in the kitchen range, put the kettle on to boil, and shoved the flatirons forward. After that she pulled up the shades in the dining room and the parlor. Usually the sunlight on the lake below blinded her so that she saw yellow circles on the geraniums and wandering jew and the slick leaves of the rubber plant, but this morning the sun was a dull red, less dazzling than a full moon.

Hattie cooked coffee and cakes and sausages and toast and eggs for the game warden and the driver of the mail truck, who lived at the hotel the year round, and for two timber cruisers who had come in from Norway. All of them ate with their noses in their plates, sipping coffee while their mouths were full, still chewing as they folded their napkins. Afterwards they filled their pockets at the toothpick bowl, and walked around digging at their gums.

Hattie had time to iron six sheets before she heard the familiar summons of a knife tapping a glass. She tucked in the loose ends of her hair and rolled down her sleeves before she went into the dining room. The girl and boy—just as she had expected. The girl's yellow head was resting in the crook of her elbow on the chairback, while she watched the boy rather languidly as he read Hattie's paper, which had come in with the mail the day before.

"According to this," said the boy, "we'd better not try to go on."

"I wouldn't try it," said Hattie, "not until the wind changes. It's burning over by Norway now."

They wanted everything, they said, coffee, cakes, sausages, toast, eggs, and as Hattie went back to the kitchen, she bumped into Alvin, who was peering through the crack at the hinge of the door.

"See here," said Hattie, "you'd better get started at the dishes."

Alvin was aggrieved, but he tied an apron around his middle and rattled the dishpans as if he were working hastily.

While the boy and girl were eating—and they took a long time about it—the other guests came down. This week they were all men, and most of them were Hattie's regular customers. Some of them, she knew, came to fish; others, like Stiegler, had some business up on the border. They never brought their wives. But they paid their bills, and generally behaved themselves, and they were decent to Hattie. Quite likely Stiegler would add a dollar or two to the bill on account of last night. They had their own way of setting their consciences at rest.

Hattie stayed in the dining room most of the time they were eating. She was a little uneasy about the girl. Girls didn't come to the Griggs Hotel.

"Wind's pretty high, Mrs. Griggs."

"Yes, sir, it is."

"We may be running for it yet. Wouldn't be the first time for me. I was in Cloquet in 1918 . . ."

They swapped stories about the big fire. "Fifteen poor fools shut themselves up in a root cellar . . ."

When they began to fold their napkins, Hattie went upstairs to do the chamber work. Soiled sheets, slop jars, bowls with gray rings where the soapy water had stood, cigarette ashes floating on the top, burned matches . . . Stiegler's door was locked. He hadn't been down for breakfast, and Hattie knew she would find a mess in there.

In No. 209 the girl was sitting on the edge of the bed, filing her nails.

"Excuse me," said Hattie.

"Come ahead," called the girl. So Hattie went in. The girl's things were spread out on the dresser, pearl-handled implements, an ivory brush with a blue initial, a lipstick . . . there must have been perfume somewhere, for the room was sweet. On the bed, dumped down any old way, Hattie found a crumpled piece of pale pink silk, set with lace medallions. It was, she knew, a nightgown. Hattie shook it and smoothed it, and folded it away in the top of an open suitcase.

"Did you say you come from Minneapolis?" asked Hattie. "Well, that's my home. I've been away from there for fourteen years."

"Honest?"

"Wait a minute," said Hattie. She went downstairs and brought back the photograph that hung over the rubber plant in the parlor. "That's our old home. It was a fine house. Stone."

"Which one is you?" asked the girl, looking at the family group arranged in tiers on the steps.

Hattie indicated the littlest girl, whose hair was held back by an Alice-in-Wonderland comb.

"When I get money enough I'm going back. I was all ready to go ten years ago, but the bank failed. I've got a timber claim up north of here that's going to be worth money someday . . . if it doesn't burn up first."

Hattie was interrupted by the telephone ringing, three short and two long. The operator's voice was shaky. "Say, they told me to warn you folks. It looks like Norway is gone. They don't answer. The wind's coming straight this way, Mrs. Griggs."

The girl, who had followed Hattie down, listened while she told the men. The girl was doing nervous things with her hands. The boy was rubbing his little mustache. They looked in dismay at the ashes which were falling everywhere like dust, very light— nothing but a streak of soot when rubbed between the thumb and forefinger.

Presently, other people came in, the town banker, the postmaster, the garageman, the doctor, the weekend guests, who had been standing outside, whistling, with their hands in their pockets. They all looked at Hattie.

"What'll you do?" asked Hattie. "Backfire?"

"If we have time," said the banker, clearing his throat. "Come on, you fellows. We've got to fight it. Carlson's place looks all right, but Peterson's gone to the city and his wife's all alone. Just her and the four kids. Where's that fellow Stiegler? Wake him up, somebody. Tell Alvin to come along . . ."

Hattie pounded on Stiegler's door until he answered. She shoved him and those two friends of his down the stairs. Alvin was yelling for her to find his coat and the axe. Hattie ran after the boy, who was starting off reluctantly. "Give me the keys to your car," she shouted.

"There now," said Hattie to the girl. "You just stay with me."

They went out to the kitchen, and part of the time they had to feel their way because the smoke was so thick. It not only shut out the sunlight, but it made their eyes water so that they couldn't see. Hattie didn't wonder the girl was scared. They could hear a roaring sound in the distance, and occasionally a crashing of trees.

"I guess I'd better get out the potatoes for dinner," said Hattie, fumbling blindly in the closet where she kept her supplies. She thought she heard the girl give a little sob, but she couldn't be sure. She began to think of all the other things that had happened—blizzards, storms that had ripped off the roof, rains that had ruined the wallpaper, mortgages, bank failures . . .

"I don't believe I can see to pare them," said Hattie.

"There's something burning out in back," cried the girl, in a panicky voice.

Hattie went out and stamped the flame from a brand deposited there by the wind. She could see other brands in the air. Sometimes they were extinguished before they fell, sometimes they weren't. Hattie wet a broom at the pump, and beat the fires out.

"You listen to me," said Hattie to the girl, whose throat and lips and hands were trembling. "You get in your car and start the engine. I'm going up after your suitcases. There isn't any use letting your pretty things burn up. I'll be down in a minute."

She had some trouble finding her way through the smoke, but she got back all right, with the suitcases and her own tin box, and the photograph of her father's home in Minneapolis.

"You drive down on the beach," she told the girl. "You can go a little way into the water, but don't get your engine wet unless you have to. This wind is as like as not to change yet. There'll be other people down on the beach, and you do just what they do. Wet your hair and hold your handkerchief over your face. And don't come back until everybody says it's safe. You may get hot, but you can't burn up out in the lake. I'll come down when I have to, and so will the men. You needn't worry about them; they'll look out for themselves."

The girl drove away nervously, a little red figure crouching to see the road.

III

Hattie found a gunnysack and soaked it in water. She ran here and there with it, smothering the fires as they started to blaze. She was nearly crazy with the smoke in her eyes. She set the ladder up against the porch, and on it she mounted to the roof to beat out a brand that had lodged on the ridgepole. While she was clinging there, trying to get her breath, Peterson's wife ran past, holding her apron over her baby. Three little children, all screaming, were running after her, pulling each other, stumbling, staggering . . .

Dimly, through the smoke, she saw Alvin coming back. His hat was gone; his cheek was bleeding, and he was breathing in a horrible way, through his mouth. Hattie climbed down, and trampled on two little fires before she reached him.

"Where's the axe?"

Alvin pointed behind him. "God, Hattie; I got hit by a tree," he gasped. Hattie felt, quickly, all around his shoulder and side.

"Nothing's broken," she shouted in his ear. "You go back and get that axe."

The sparks were falling all around them as they used to fall on Fourth of July nights a long time ago from Roman candles. A piece of wood no bigger than Hattie's thumb fell on the broad branch of a spruce tree behind her, and immediately the needles sizzled and blazed and shriveled. Then the next limb caught and the next.

Alvin sat down on the wooden platform by the pump. Hattie ran into the grove, looking for the axe. She tripped once, over a root she didn't see, and fell on her stomach on a pile of brush. And while she was lying there, stupid, choking, she saw the glitter of the axe blade, not ten feet away. Somehow or other she found her way back and began hacking at the trunk of a white pine that stood between the blaze and the kitchen porch. It fell, after a while, and one of its branches shattered a kitchen window.

Hattie was standing by the pump, heaving and choking, when she noticed something . . . It happened very quietly, as if it were nothing of the least importance . . . only this . . . the sparks began to fly north instead of east. Hattie watched the smoke clouds halt and turn and spread out into dirty streaks over the tops of the pines. North . . . wouldn't you know it would go north! There was nothing there but timber . . . nobody would fight it up there. It would burn itself out, tree by tree, dollar by dollar . . .

Soon the men came back, dirty, scorched, torn, scratched, bruised, sweating, breathing hard. The boy's hair had been on fire. He had lost his eyebrows and one side of his little mustache. He held his hands stiffly in front of him, and he looked at them as if very much surprised about something.

Hattie told him where he could find the girl, and then she went into the kitchen. She had to build the fire in the range all over again. She put the kettle on to boil. It occurred to her that she had just time, while the water was heating, to clean up Stiegler's room.

It proved to be even more of a mess than she had supposed. From time to time as she scrubbed, she looked out toward the north. Under the sky more fiery than the fire itself, the black smoke was writhing and coiling. Treetops blazed suddenly and disappeared. Brands fell like comets. Confused with this was a memory of the girl's white hand hanging like a blossom from her arm, with the jewel gleaming red and blue and orange in the lamplight.

With a slop pail in each hand, Hattie went downstairs.

"How about dinner?" called Alvin, as she stepped out into the yard. "Aren't we going to get no dinner today?"

Allie

One day, when I was a little girl, my mother came home in the greatest excitement. She said that Mr. Wright had run off with all the money in his bank . . . and what was going to become of Allie? She said it was bad enough for a girl to grow up without any mother, and lose her lover in a train wreck, without having this to happen.

After that we were all a little afraid of Allie. I don't mean that we suspected her of stealing—she was the kind that wouldn't hurt a fly—but we didn't know what to say to her when we met her anywhere. If we sat next to her at the soda fountain in the drugstore, for instance, we didn't like to say, "Nice day, Miss Allie," or "Will you buy a couple of tickets to the senior play?" because it didn't seem appropriate to say such things to a girl whose lover had been pinned under a Pullman car and roasted alive and whose father was a fugitive from justice. It didn't seem adequate. And then, if you said "a couple of tickets," as you were sure to from long habit, why, you were just rubbing it in. For when Allie went anywhere, she went alone.

She lived in a furnished room over the drugstore, and ate most of her meals at the soda fountain. She said it was the cheapest place in town, and of course she didn't have any money because the bank creditors took the house and everything Mr. Wright had left behind. Allie got a job as clerk in Mr. Stickney's dry goods store. Mr. Stickney put her at the notion counter, which was in a dark corner under the stairs. Even on bright days they had to keep the electric light burning, though Allie said it gave her a headache. And her back hurt because she had to stand up all the time. Everybody said it must be awful for Allie when you remember all the things she used to have.

We girls used to march along through town, with our arms on each other's shoulders, singing. Every now and then we'd meet Allie Wright going home from work. She had the funniest way of walking without swinging her arms. They just hung down, and her black cotton gloves looked as if they were stuffed with sand. I don't believe she ever bought any new clothes. She kept on wearing the clothes her father had bought for her when he was in the bank. We were always afraid, when we passed her like that, that she was going to cry. And we always stopped singing when we saw her.

"How do, Miss Allie?"

"Good evening."

It was just as if a cloud had blown over the sun.

The worst of it was that she knew how we felt. So we were always trying to make it up to her. When our Sunday School teacher moved away, we begged Allie to take our class. We said, "Please, please, Miss Allie. We'd rather have you than anybody." Of course, we wouldn't have asked her to chaperone a party or anything like that, but Sunday School didn't matter so much. We didn't go there for fun. Besides, it made us feel as if we were doing a lot of good.

Once Allie invited us up to her room over the drugstore. It was supposed to be a party. Some of the girls had dates, but we made them come anyway. It would have been too awful if they hadn't. Her room was about ten feet square, and it didn't have anything in it except a cot and a golden oak dresser and one of those small square tables on legs that slant outwards and have brass claws at the bottom, and a lot of chairs she had borrowed from the drugstore—the kind with wire backs that stick into you, and wire legs. She had a picture of her dead lover on the dresser, and we all took turns fixing our hair so that we could look at him. Afterwards we agreed that he didn't look like much, but you can never tell.

Allie

Allie wanted it to be a very gay party. We played charades and
"Twenty Questions" and "Pass the Ring," and she called us "dear,"
and smiled at us, and hoped we'd have lots of good times together.
Later she showed us some picture postals she had, and a silk handkerchief somebody had sent her from Japan, with a mountain painted on
it, and a red wineglass that said "World's Fair, Chicago" in white
letters. At half past nine she served ice cream from the drugstore and
cake from the bakery. Because it was a Sunday School party she
thought we ought to bow our heads and say a little prayer before
going home.

I was never so glad to get away from anywhere in my life. We
all went down to another drugstore and had chocolate nut sundaes,
with marshmallow sauce, and we made so much noise laughing and
singing that they nearly put us out. But all the time we remembered
how excited and happy Allie had been when she kissed us good-bye.
That kind of spoiled our fun.

II

A year or two after that, she got married. Mr. Stickney, of all people!
He was ever so much older than she, and a widower, and his reputation wasn't any too good. There was a lot of talk about them. Some
people thought it was wonderful of him to marry Allie, when he
didn't have to. Other people said it was no such thing, and anybody
could see that the baby came before its time by looking at its little
fingernails. They said it was a shame to talk like that about Allie.
After that we all managed to get a look at the baby's fingernails when
we met Allie wheeling him in his buggy, and because we felt guilty
about it, we'd say, "He has such darling little fingers, Miss Allie."

"Do you notice how long they are?" she would ask us. "And
how they taper. The palmistry book says that's a sign of genius."

Allie certainly was crazy about that baby.

The Stickney house was the ugliest in the world—one of those
gingerbread houses, with spires and wooden filigree all over it—very

27

tall and narrow, standing all by itself in the middle of the block, without a tree or a bush around it. Inside, it was dark, and cold, because the furnace wouldn't draw. All the furnishings had belonged to the first Mrs. Stickney. The first thing you saw when you went in was one of those things made of bamboo straw that people used to hang in doorways. I don't know what you call them. It always rustled when you went through. The rugs were a fright, and so was the furniture. There must have been a ton of bric-a-brac.

As her baby grew older, Allie began to go out to places. She told my mother that she owed it to Lloyd. That was what she had named him—Lloyd, because she thought it was pretty. She nearly killed herself serving church suppers and selling tickets for lectures and organizing classes to study the budget system. That was all right, but finally she started going to parties. She always came the first of all, in a dress from Stickney's that was about twenty years too young. She was so solemn and so polite that it made us all uncomfortable.

You see, we had reason to feel sorry for her again because her marriage wasn't very happy. The whole town knew that Mr. Stickney had taken his stenographer to New York with him on a buying trip. One of our men had seen them at Rector's all dolled up and drinking. He never went anywhere with Allie, and he didn't even stay at home evenings. The neighbors told a lot about what went on.

So that was one reason why we hated to see her at a party. It was just the way it had been before: we didn't know what to talk about. Other people talked about their husbands and the latest show and where they were going on their vacations, but the only safe topic with Allie was Lloyd, and that got to be a bore because Allie didn't know where to stop. She worshipped him so much that she kind of choked up while she talked.

And her bridge! Heavens! She used to get her hearts in with her diamonds, she dropped cards, she got mixed up on the deal, and when she made a wrong play—well, it was pitiful. Her face and ears and neck would turn dark red and we would all hold our breaths for fear she was going to cry. She'd say, "I'm awfully sorry . . . I can't understand how it happened," and we'd say, "Oh, that's all right. We're just playing for the fun of it, anyway." But we were always glad to move on.

When Lloyd was about ten years old, a dreadful thing happened. Mr. Stickney died of heart failure. I don't mean that his dying was so dreadful, but the place where he died . . . with that woman and all! And the whole story coming out on the front page! We hadn't had such a scandal since Mr. Wright ran off with the bank funds. Of course we had to call on Allie, two or three of us at a time, and believe me, that was an ordeal. It didn't seem just right to say nice things about him, so we talked rather vaguely about how bravely she bore up under her troubles and how we did wish we could do something. "My son is my great comfort," Allie kept saying.

Nobody knew why Lloyd was such a comfort, especially when he grew older. He was a sort of moody boy, who didn't do well in high school, and wasn't very popular. In some ways he was like his father; he never went anywhere with his mother, or seemed to pay any attention to her. She baked cakes for him, and gave him a bigger allowance than any of the other boys, and even bought a car, which he drove everywhere. I doubt if she rode in it more than once.

III

One day she dropped in to see me on her way downtown. I could see she was tickled about something, and pretty soon she told me. She had found a poem on Lloyd's dresser, scribbled on a scrap of paper. "I can't help but feel," she said, "that Lloyd is a born writer. He has always been a remarkable child, though I am sorry to say he hasn't been appreciated. Listen to this:

> I have been here before,
> But when or how I cannot tell:
> I knew the grass beyond the door. . . ."

I think that's the way it went. Of course, I told her I thought it

29

was lovely and that she ought to be proud of him, but all the time I
had the funniest feeling about it. I don't really know how to describe
it, except that I felt more sorry for her when she was happy than
when she wasn't. It depressed me just terribly. For her to get all excited because Lloyd wrote a poem! . . . He was so homely, and so—
oh, morbid, I guess you'd call it.

I told the other girls about it, and they almost killed themselves
being nice to her. They'd say, "Well, I hear Lloyd is awfully tal-
ented. We always knew he'd amount to a lot, Mrs. Stickney." And
then, as likely as not, they'd wink at each other behind her back.
That was sort of mean, but you can't blame them much. And she
never suspected anything.

Lloyd lived up to his reputation, all right. At least he left poems
around his room. Allie used to copy them and learn them by heart,
but she didn't mention them to Lloyd. She said it was too sacred.
She said he had the artistic temperament, anybody could see that;
he was so sensitive, and he liked to be by himself. She said she used
to watch for his light to go out, and sometimes it would be two in
the morning before he went to bed. She wouldn't have disturbed
him for anything while he was writing.

When Allie had collected about a hundred poems, she had an
idea. She thought of it in the night, and she came down right after
breakfast to consult me about it. "It's that Literary Club program,"
she explained. "You know the club meets with me next month . . ."

I knew that all right, because I had been on the program com-
mittee, and we had given her the meeting just before Christmas,
when almost everybody was too busy to come.

"Now, I've an idea," she went on. "It means a great deal to me.
Don't you think the ladies would appreciate it if I read them Lloyd's
poems? It don't seem right," she said, "for us to neglect our own
talent, and Lloyd needs encouragement so bad. I know a little recognition would mean a lot to him. And the ladies might be interested enough to help him get his work published. I haven't had

much education," she said, "but nobody could help thinking that Lloyd's poems are lovely."

Well, I didn't know what to do. I asked her if Lloyd knew about the plan, and she said no, that he was so sensitive that she didn't suppose he would ever consent to it. "But when he finds out how much you all like them," she kept saying . . . and I said, "Oh, yes, I'm sure the ladies will like them." I just had to let her go ahead. The rest of us agreed to go, and be nice, and praise his poems up to the skies, although we were all counting on a good laugh when we got home.

So Allie cleaned her house and trimmed it up for the great day. It was so near Christmas that she used holly and ground pine and mistletoe, and so much of it that the bric-a-brac was hidden and the place looked almost pretty for once. She lighted all the gas grates to make it cheery, and she stood in the hall in a new red dress with lots of gold trimming and little gold buttons up and down the front. She was all aflutter.

We tried not to look at each other when she started the program. She made a little speech about Lloyd, and then she began to read the poems. They had funny names, like "To a Waterfowl" and "Break, Break, Break," and she didn't know how to pronounce all the words. And of course she read abominably. One of them was about something called a nautilus, and I've always wondered about that because it sounded like a poem I read a long time ago in school. Maybe not, though. We all sat there with our hands in our laps, trying to look soulful. Once or twice I nearly laughed, but on the whole we were behaving ourselves pretty well when a funny thing happened.

Lloyd came in the front door. Allie didn't hear him. She was reading: "At midnight, in the silence of the sleep time / When you set your fancies free. . . ." When she got to the end, she stopped and said, "Ladies, can you imagine what it means to a mother to have her son write lines like these? Ladies, when I found these lines

I have been reading to you in my son's room, I fell down on my knees and thanked God that He had made it possible."

IV

Lloyd stood in the hall behind the bamboo curtain, and everybody saw him except Allie. Afterwards I thought we ought to have called him in and congratulated him, or something like that, but he looked so wild and funny that none of us said a word. Allie picked up another poem. "I think Lloyd must have been listening to a bird when he wrote this," she said. "Hark! ah, the nightingale— / The tawny-throated . . ."

Lloyd stared and stared. He didn't seem to see any of us except his mother. His face was perfectly awful, dead white, and all puckered around his mouth. Before she finished, he went out, and we heard him go down the front steps.

"I'm not going to read any more," said Allie, "but if any of the ladies wish to look them over . . ."

The rest is so dreadful that I hardly know how to tell it. Allie was passing the refreshments, all trembly and proud and wiping her eyes, when a man ran into the house. Of course, he didn't know which was Allie, and so he blurted out: "A boy has just shot himself down here. They're taking him to the hospital, though I guess it ain't much use . . . Right through the head."

We all looked at Allie. Somebody screamed and a lot of us began to cry. She didn't move, not even her eyes. She just stood staring at that man with her mouth half open. If it had been anyone but Allie, we would have gone up to her and kissed her and patted her hands and tried to comfort her. But we couldn't . . . with Allie. I suppose we all remembered how we had laughed about the poems, and how we always hated to have her around on account of all the troubles she had had.

The man said, "Come with me. My car's just outside," and he

led her out of the house. She walked like one of those dolls you see sometimes. Only her feet moved. The rest of her was like wood.

And there we sat, feeling perfectly awful, but not doing a thing.

The last I saw of Allie was that hideous red dress being hoisted into the man's car.

"For goodness sake!" I said. "She's forgot her dress!"

Of course, I meant to say that she had forgotten her coat, and everybody knew it. There wasn't anything funny about it, either. But we were all so keyed up about it that we began to giggle.

We didn't look at each other, because I suppose we were the least little bit ashamed. I remember biting my lips and chewing my handkerchief, but I couldn't stop giggling. After a minute we put on our wraps and ran home, not in groups, as we usually did, but one by one. And when I opened my front door, and saw the babies playing in front of the fire, all safe and sound, I flopped down on the floor and had regular hysterics. I couldn't help it.

And now, whenever I see Allie coming, I can't help remembering how we sat in her house and laughed. Probably that's why I always cross the street to avoid meeting her. I wouldn't know what to say.

Saved

Willard sat in a folding chair in the second row, his arms crossed and his feet sunk in the sawdust. On his right sat his mother, who reached up to her neck now and then to crease down the collar of her starched Mother Hubbard. On his left sat a tall woman with no lap, and thighs which might have been marble under her tightly drawn skirt. She held a handkerchief, neatly folded, which smelled of lilies of the valley.

While the evangelist waited, his forehead in his hand, the choir sang very, very softly, "Jesus, Lover of My Soul." The song leader tiptoed back and forth in front of them, holding back the sound with his arms, tossing his long, wavy hair out of his eyes.

The lilies of the valley reminded Willard of Myrtle. He could smell the drugstore and see the bottles of perfume tilted in their boxes, each crowned by a cap of white kid, and Myrtle's finger pointing to this and to that while she said to a customer, "How'd you like rose now, dearie?" For Myrtle had been selling perfume the first time he had seen her, and he had watched her while he waited for his mother's prescription. But he had been afraid to speak to her . . . then.

Tonight, after the meeting, he would make some excuse to his mother, and he would call at the drugstore for Myrtle. He knew how secretly she would look at him as she took down her hat. Out on the sidewalk she would snuggle up while he took her arm, and would say, "Oh, honey, I'm dead tired tonight," as they strolled toward her rooming house.

The choir began "In the Swee-ee-eet Bye and Bye." The voices slid plaintively, deliciously, from note to note. A hundred cardboard fans beat the air, keeping time, and the lilies of the valley blew toward Willard in little gusts. The scalloped edge of the tent flapped in the hot wind; the long strings of electric lights swayed back and forth. Willard, as excited as if Myrtle were close to him, squirmed, and wiped his wet palms with his handkerchief.

When the piano began "Alas! And Did My Savior Bleed?" the evangelist raised his head. Willard didn't feel like singing. He stood, not too erect, with his hands resting on the back of the chair in front, and wondered if Myrtle would like the bracelets he had bought for her. He had held back a dollar from the wages he turned over to his mother so that he might buy six of them, of various colors, intended to be worn all together on one arm. Willard shivered as he imagined them on Myrtle's white arm. They would shake down to her elbow when she threw up her arms and Willard supposed they would tinkle a little. Maybe he would feel them pressing into the back of his neck. He would kiss Myrtle, if he felt like it, under the ear.

> At the cross, at the cross,
> Where I first saw the light,
> And the burden of my heart rolled away. . . .

Willard shifted feet. He wished it would stop. It was like seeing Myrtle behind the counter without being able to touch her.

The prayer was better because he didn't have to listen. Instead, he looked around. He saw old Mr. Palmer leaning forward so that his cheek rested on his cane and his whiskers covered his hands. He saw Mrs. Herman, with her seven little girls, and the baby at her breast. He saw people he didn't know tiptoeing out with crying babies over their shoulders.

> Hallelujah! Thine the glory!
> Hallelujah! Amen!

36

Hallelujah! Thine the glory!
Revive us again!

Myrtle's voice, pleading, "If we could only be . . . you know
. . . married!" And his own voice, shrill in spite of his efforts to keep
it down, "Well, you see I promised Mama I wouldn't until I was
twenty-one."

Myrtle had said, "Two years, duckie!"

And he had said, "That's too long for us, you baby, you sweet
baby." Myrtle had cried for some reason when he had taken hold
of her.

II

Now they were singing "Shall We Gather at the River," the ladies
first, then the gentlemen, then together, with the song leader's voice
topping the rest triumphantly . . . "Yes, we'll gather at the river . . ."
The music brought back the funeral of Willard's little sister, years
ago, the perfume of carnations, the unbearable sound of his mother's sobbing, and, for no reason he understood, Myrtle's hands reaching for his across the table in her room. It was the first night she had
let him come. Myrtle had taken two bottles of ginger ale from the
drugstore to accompany Willard's first pint of corn liquor. They had
not wanted to be wicked so much as courageous, able to forget for
once Willard's shrill voice and his sallow skin and the sleaziness of
Myrtle's silk stockings. So they had sipped their highballs quite
jauntily for a time, until Myrtle had held out her hands and said,
almost crying, "I don't believe we had better drink any more, honey."
Willard had laughed.

The audience was getting settled for the sermon. The choir
laid aside the hymnbooks, the leader smoothed back his hair and
folded his arms complacently, the evangelist rose slowly to his feet.
He was a powerful man with brilliant eyes which sifted the audience
person by person, and rested at last on Willard. "Brother," said the

preacher, leaning across the reading stand and pointing his finger directly at Willard. "Brother, where are you going to spend eternity? In Heaven with the angels? or in that place of which it is said, 'Their worm dieth not and the fire is not quenched'?"

Once Myrtle had sobbed as someone behind him was sobbing now. "Dearie, sometimes I'm scared," she had whispered.

Willard hadn't known what to answer because he was himself scared. He was crazy about her, just crazy . . . and yet he was afraid. Sixteen dollars a week . . . and his mother. And he didn't have luck like the other fellows. Besides, Myrtle wasn't his mother's kind; she wouldn't want to scrub and shovel coal and clean up after boarders. "Dearie, sometimes I'm scared."

"Aw, cut it out," he had said.

That was the night when he had carried away Myrtle's little comb, a red comb which folded into a celluloid case, such a comb as girls used for their bobbed hair. Myrtle had run it through his hair that night while he sat on the floor with his head in her lap. She had tied red tissue paper over the electric light bulb because the room became, then, dim and mysterious, like the love scenes in the movies. In that ruddy light they might have been anywhere. The water dripping in the bathtub down the hall might have been a fountain in a garden. Everything was different.

"I'll make a lot of money some of these days," Willard had boasted, and he had believed it at the time. "And we'll go to Paris, shall we?"

"Willard, I want to go so bad that sometimes I cry. I do, honest. When I see Gloria Swanson's clothes and the way she walks, with her head like a queen's . . . Oh, Willard, I just can't stand it for always in this town. You don't think it's bad, do you?—to want clothes and things?"

"Naw!" Willard had told her. "And I'll buy them for you, too, if I ever get my chance. Only you've got to be a good kid and not like anybody but me."

"I won't . . . ever," Myrtle had promised. "Not anybody but you. You've been awful sweet to me. You're all I've got."

Willard had taken the comb away in his pocket, and when he had gone to bed in the little room that opened from his mother's kitchen, he had taken it out and combed his own hair, trying to recall the illusion of that earlier hour. He had failed, of course, without Myrtle or the red tissue paper, and in disgust he had let the comb drop to the floor, where his mother had found it in the morning. She had said, "Willard, where did you get that thing?"

"I found it in the street," he had answered. But he knew by the gingerly way she picked it up and threw it out among the tin cans that she didn't believe him.

All through breakfast she had been silent, occasionally wiping her eyes on her apron. But when Willard got up, she had said, "You leave women alone, do you hear? It was women ruined your papa . . . women and drink."

That had happened a month or more ago. Slowly Willard came back to the present scene. The evangelist was talking about sins. One by one he was checking them off. Greed, the lust for money, for power, the lure of the gambling den, fine clothes, silk stockings, Paris. Willard looked down at his trousers, which flared at the bottom, and his shiny yellow shoes . . . "where their worm dieth not . . ." He rubbed his chin, smooth from the razor, and found it clammy like rubber.

Strong drink . . . the cup that polluteth. Old Mr. Palmer sighed and groaned at the description of the drunkard, bleary-eyed, filthy, staggering home through the night to his wife and babies. Willard's father had come home drunk once or twice, bleary-eyed, perhaps, but very happy. Willard remembered seeing him lurch into the bedroom and sit down on the bed to laugh. He had told some very funny stories. He had been generous, too, to the extent of handing Willard's mother a five-dollar bill.

Willard's mother had said, "Ain't I got enough to stand without your coming home drunk? Ain't I, now? Shaming yourself before your son, too. And I wearing my fingers to the bone over the washing and the cooking." His father had laughed at that until he had fallen over onto the pillow. But Willard's mother had never forgotten it, and when his father was dying with that cancer in his stomach, she told him over and over again, "You have no one to thank for this but yourself . . . you and your liquor and your women."

The preacher reached Myrtle at last. To save his soul Willard could not get away from his eyes. He dodged behind Mr. Palmer, and Mr. Palmer leaned forward to spit in the sawdust. He tried looking at the string of electric lights, but the rhythm of their swaying made him feel sick. He examined his fingernails and the end of his necktie and the toes of his yellow oxfords, but all the time he knew that the evangelist was watching him. He had to look up in the end. All over the tent men were coughing and women were crying . . . The dance . . . the seduction of painted lips . . . a kiss . . . the arms of the scarlet woman . . .

He had danced with Myrtle . . . admission fifty cents and ladies free. They had been one body instead of two. He had been conscious at first of her hand and the muscles of her back, but he had forgotten her altogether after a while, and had known only that he liked to dance.

The preacher's finger beat in time to his words. "Sinners! Let me say it again. Listen to the prophecy . . . 'where their worm dieth not and the fire is not quenched.' . . . Brother, will that be said of you?" He began pointing here and there in the audience. "Of you? . . . of you? . . . of you?"

It seemed to Willard that the lilies of the valley became a hundred times more penetrating; the scalloped edge of the tent flapped more violently; the cardboard fans increased the frenzy of their rhythm; the strings of lights swung back and forth as if some human emotion were beating through the wire.

He pointed at Willard last of all. For an instant Willard thought he had spoken his name. He felt that he ought to get up out of his

40

chair, like a man he had seen hypnotized at a show once—get up and walk straight toward that motionless finger. It dropped at last and the speaker's voice changed. He was pleading now, coaxing, praying for repentance. "Brother, will you come and confess your sins? Will you let Him wash them away? Can you deny Him? Dare you deny Him?"

Willard's whole body was wet with perspiration. So furiously was the blood beating behind his eyes that the evangelist became a blur, distorted, gigantic. The voice rose again . . . "Come! you who believe, you who would be saved, come to the Mercy Seat."

III

The meeting dissolved in tears and prayers and stumbling creatures crowding forward. The woman on Willard's left pushed past him, and took away with her the lilies of the valley. Willard noticed the bulging of her breast and the surprising slenderness of her ankles. He shuddered.

> There is a fountain filled with blood,
> Drawn from Emmanuel's veins,
> And Sinners plunged beneath its flood
> Lose all their guilty stains. . . .

Old Mr. Palmer was crying. He had no handkerchief and the tears ran down on his mohair coat. Willard saw, drunkenly, the loose skin of his cheeks, and the creases, diamond-shaped, like a lattice, in his neck. Disgust rose in his throat. His own hands, he realized, were soft and flabby. He was ashamed of them, and of his face smooth like a girl's. Myrtle had put her hands on his cheeks. "Love me, kid?" he had asked her, huskily.

"You bet."

Willard knelt in the sawdust. The tears were running between his fingers down his wrists, under the cuffs of his shirt. Over him floated the muted voices of the choir.

Just as I am,
      Without one plea,
But that Thy blood
      Was shed for me. . . .

When he reached for his handkerchief, the six little bracelets rolled out of his pocket and lay gleaming on the sawdust.

"God, Mama!" said Willard hoarsely. "There *was* a woman!"

The Monument

Before dawn the baby began to cry. Margaret lifted her out of her crib and sat down in the low rocker by the open window. Back and forth she rocked, but ever so slightly, for the chair had a habit of squeaking and she musn't disturb the older children. Polly snuggled her cheek, slippery with tears, in her mother's neck.

Margaret wasn't sleepy and she wasn't tired, but she moved in the curious, dreamlike state that had become habitual since Richard's death. Was grief like this to everyone? She didn't know, really, though she had supposed it was more bitter. She didn't feel like herself at all—more like a spirit moving in familiar places. While Richard was alive, little things had irritated her; she had been impatient with the children sometimes, and even a little sorry for herself after a difficult day. Now the trifles didn't matter; she glided through the weeks, hardly conscious of their passing. She only knew that she must keep on gliding, that she musn't stop for an instant or the flood she was holding back with all the tenseness of her body would pour down and drown them all. Sometimes there was a little break in her dam. That puzzled the children. Why did Mother cry when she absentmindedly set an extra plate at the table? Or when the telephone happened to ring just before five in the afternoon?

The night was warm. The moon had turned the grass in the back yard to a tender gold. A single ray ventured into the bedroom and chose for its abiding place the scattered curls on Polly's head— the curls and just the tip of her tiny nose. Her mother leaned her head against the chairback, shut her eyes, and rocked in short, regular measure, like the ticking of a clock. "Tick-tack, tick-tack," went the rocker.

"What are you doing, Mama?"

"Rocking Polly, darling. Shut your eyes and go back to sleep."

It was quiet at night, too quiet. She liked the daytime better, when one was busy. At night there was nothing to do except think— except remember, rather. Lately her mind hadn't functioned well. She wanted to think, to work out a theory for this business of living and dying, but her mind refused to do anything except remember. I'm getting positively morbid, she reproved herself.

Richard had gone, and she was here: that was all. And now Polly was limp and asleep in her arms. She laid the child in her crib, giving her the lightest possible kiss on her warm forehead. Little darling, little darling.

She stepped softly across the floor to Ted. On top of the blanket, of course, you rascal. He reached a sturdy arm about her neck and drew down her lips.

"Good night," she whispered.

" 'Night."

Spirit-like she moved through the room. She must look at Virginia, sleeping so daintily in the moon-bright alcove, her yellow braids hanging down from the bedside like tasseled cords, and at Dick in the small room beyond. His shaggy, dark head looked like a curled-up puppy on the pillow. She closed his door, and went down the hall to her mother's room. No need to go in, for she could hear from outside the old lady's gentle snoring. On the way back to her own room she turned the hall light out. Boarders were careless, and, oh misery, to have to be so parsimonious; but how hard it was to find the pennies that made the dollars!

Back in bed. Her bed. Their bed. It was a solid bed, mahogany, and Richard had bought it before they were married. They had been delightfully embarrassed about buying it, and afraid to look at each other. Little scenes had a way lately of detaching themselves

from her memory and pushing into the limelight of her conscious-
ness, queer little scenes, sentimental little scenes, sometimes quite
stupid little scenes almost forgotten. For instance: Richard and Margaret, lying in this same bed, not so very long after their marriage,
perhaps a year, for they were already planning for Dick, and Margaret
turning to him suddenly in a panic, when he was nearly asleep.

"Richard, I'm afraid."

"Afraid!" Richard was never afraid of anything, even dying.

"Yes, I am. Afraid for all the things that are going to happen to
us. Richard, people die, and people's children die. Dreadful things
happen, and they'll happen to us."

"Yes, they do; I suppose they do happen. But they can't take
back what we've had already." He kissed her. "But I don't mind saying, just this once, that I dread being old, Margo, old and helpless
and doddering and slopping my food. By George, I should mind
that."

Richard hadn't lived to be old and helpless and doddering and
slopping his food. Three months ago he had died, right here in this
bed, where Margaret was lying now. That scene she could not forget. It crowded in sometimes between her and the dinner table; it
rose up in the street as she passed. His face in the pillow, strangely
yellow, except around the mouth where the set teeth made it white,
his black eyes following her around like the painted eyes in clever
advertisements, his thin hand gripping the blanket. "I know you'll
manage, Margo, I know that; but I wish to God I had been able to
make it easier." No sentimentality, for all his tenderness. No apolo-
gies. Not from Richard.

Margaret threw back the heavy braid of her hair and closed her
eyes. Back came sleep, like a warm, dark cloud.

Ted woke her in the morning.

Polly gurgled in the crib. There was a flutter of bedclothes, and
two pink feet began kicking heartily. Margaret got up. She dressed
quickly and coiled her rich brown hair into a knot at the back.

Virginia dried the breakfast dishes.

"Is it today you're going to Mrs. Chalmers's?"

"Yes."

"Mama, is she very rich?"

"Very."

"As rich as we are?"

"Much richer, dear."

"How many children has she?"

"Only one, Jinny. His name is Jack. He's Dick's age."

"When I grow up I'm going to have ten children, five boys and five girls." A crash. "Oh, Mama!"

"Oh, the pink cream pitcher, Jinny. Father gave it to me for Christmas when you were a baby. Poor little pitcher. Don't cry, child; let's sweep up the pieces. Don't cry; it doesn't matter. There's no use being sentimental about pitchers. They always break, and we have so many other things to . . ."

"Mama, do you remember the time Father cooked dinner when you were sick? And he burned the potatoes? And it was all such a joke? And Dick laughed so hard he fell out of his chair?"

"There, my dear, that's all. Take Ted out in the yard with you to play. Only be sure the gates are shut tight."

The meals had to be planned, the groceries ordered, the potatoes put in the oven for the children's lunch. Busy, busy life! All the time she was wondering what she would write for her column in Saturday's paper.

Before she changed her dress she went to her mother's room. Grandmother was sitting by the window, crocheting. She crocheted endlessly, and pulled it out, and began again, quite content. Grandmother's mind had gone to its reward long ago; her body had been left behind, forgotten. Margaret sat down on the smooth edge of the bed. Grandmother's room was quiet, the only room in the house where one could be wholly at rest. Grandmother didn't see one at all, didn't talk.

Margaret began to wonder about her visit to Julia Chalmers. What would they have to say to each other? With Richard she had gone to Mr. Chalmers's funeral, only a month or two before Richard himself was buried; and she had pressed Richard's arm tightly on the way home and whispered, "You won't give me a high church funeral, will you, dear?" And he had laughed and said, "Of course not; you can count on its being altogether informal and jolly." Everyone had thought Richard's funeral so peculiar. The baby had gurgled happily, and Ted had insisted on hugging his green cloth dog. Only Virginia, in the shelter of Dick's arm, had sobbed appropriately. Browning's "Prospice," which Richard was old-fashioned enough to like, and "Lead, Kindly Light," because he used to sing it so lustily on Sunday nights.

Of course, Julia considered herself bound to Richard in a very special way. Once, for a whole year, they had been engaged. And because she had been the one to break it Julia always acted as if she had to make it up to him. Richard was amused by it. "Oh, let her think I feel that way, Margo; it gives her a lot of pleasure."

She dressed hurriedly. Her hair was so contrary that she had to put it up three times before she was satisfied. The dark serge dress was rather warm, but she really had nothing else suitable. Be thankful it isn't a scorching hot day. Good, there was the girl she had hired to stay with the children. It meant that she would have to do next week's washing herself, but never mind. She couldn't say no to Julia, even to save a dollar.

"Hello, Ted," she heard Mina saying. "What a big boy. Yes, that's a big boat. Where you sail him?"

"Can I come in, Mother?"

"May I, Dick; not can I."

"May I come in, then?"

"Certainly, if you'll find the clothes brush and brush me off. That's it, son, now the back. Do I look all right?"

47

"You're always a good-looker. Pretty as a parrot in pink per-cale—" Some of his father's nonsense. Dick stopped for fear that he might be hurting her.

"I haven't heard that for ages, Dick. How you do remember things."

"Oh, rats, Mother. Pull your hat over your nose. Look sporty for once. Now you'll take the prize."

"Good-bye, dears, all of you. Mina will get your lunch. Don't forget the baby's bottle, Mina, or Ted's nap. Good-bye."

She had to run half a block for the streetcar, and all her change was at the very bottom of her purse, under everything. Just one seat left, thank heaven for it. Julia lived at the end of nowhere, the Chalmers estate, and estates were not planned to accommodate passengers of streetcars. Margaret walked half a mile up a curving driveway which led, at last, to a porte cochere. The maid looked at her as if she were a servant in search of employment. Margaret had to say, "I am expected for lunch."

She was ushered into the vast living room she had seen once before. She hated it. It was massive and gorgeous and in perfect order. Was Julia going to kiss her? Probably; that was part of the etiquette of death, though why one should desire indiscriminate kisses at such a time she could not imagine.

She didn't even hear Julia coming until her heel clicked on the bare floor between two Oriental rugs.

"Oh, Margaret, my dear."

"Why, Julia."

The kiss, of course, chilly and damp. Julia was in black, most unbecomingly. Her face was swollen and powdered, as if she had tried to cover up the signs of weeping.

"My poor girl, you too."

"Julia, did you come to his funeral? Did you mind the baby's laughing? She's so little, you know, and she saw the plume on Mrs. Lawson's hat."

How perfectly absurd. She mustn't go on like that. But what

48

could she talk about? One couldn't suddenly switch to clothes or the weather. Julia looked disturbed. She put her handkerchief to her eyes.

"To think that Richard should have to go too."

"Oh, I'm so glad he didn't have to be old. He dreaded that, you know." She simply musn't give in to Julia.

"Yes, to be old and alone . . . You and I . . ."

"Nonsense, Julia, we're not forty yet. Where's Jack? I'd like to see him."

"He will join us in a few minutes. You know, Margaret, he feels much as I do. We had never dreamed of such a tragedy."

"Haven't you really, Julia, with people dying every day?"

Julia shuddered. "Don't! Don't!" After a silence. "And your children?"

"Oh, they are such darlings. Polly can sit up alone now, and Ted—well, you'd hardly believe he could be so big. And Virginia is such a dear and Dick is going to be his father all over again. When I was dressing he said 'Pretty as a parrot in pink percale.'"

Julia's bleak face was tinged with a mournful surprise, as if she didn't want to be surprised—wasn't interested in surprise or anything else—but couldn't help herself this time. Margaret bit her lip. I'm being an idiot, she thought, babbling nonsense like this, but I'm not going to pull down my flag. Never.

Jack came in just as lunch was announced. He was a large child with a timorous bearing, and he had a pathetic way of glancing at his mother for permission before he said or did anything. He shook hands feebly. Margaret didn't know what to say to him. They went into the dining room.

"How is Dick?" he asked in a dull voice.

"Oh, he has a radio set, Jack, and he does have the best time with it. His father helped him build it the last thing before he . . ." Jack looked frightened. She was evidently about to say something that wasn't said on the Chalmers estate. I will say it, she told herself, I'm not afraid of it. " . . . the last thing before he died." Silence.

Jack turned his eyes away. "It wasn't quite finished, you know, but Dick got a book from the library, and I tried to help though I wasn't much good, being a woman; still, I could hold the wires while he soldered. And when it was all in order we tuned in and heard Schenectady the very first thing."

"Jack has a set," Julia said, "but we haven't had the heart for it, since—February, of course."

"We use Dick's all the time. You know, Virginia is ambitious to play the violin, and when she comes across a concert we all have to whisper and step around like kittens for fear she'll miss a strain. Dick keeps a list of all the stations he hears, and he says he's going to visit every single one before he dies." Unfortunate word; Julia winced.

"I intended to travel a good deal." Margaret positively jumped at the grown-up disillusioned voice Jack assumed. Well, he probably would; he was immensely rich. And Dick probably wouldn't, for the contrary reason; but even so, Dick would have ten times as much honest-to-goodness joy, just talking about it.

She told them of the treasure island that Dick had picked out on the map, after reading an account of the Spanish adventurers, and of the picture of it that Virginia had painted for his birthday, with two palms at each end and a log cabin in between.

"Imagine it, Jack, logs on a desert island. She even had a pirate flag, with the most horrible skull and crossbones you can imagine." Heavens, there she had put her foot in it again. Couldn't Julia think of anything except the ugly side of death? Couldn't she even mention pirate flags?

They all ate sparingly. Margaret was sure the Chalmerses ate only as a matter of convention, never from hunger. And as for herself, she could hardly swallow for the swelling in her throat. She had made a great mistake in coming, of course.

Afterwards Jack said good-bye and disappeared. "Lie down for an hour," his mother told him, "and then you may go for a drive."

Margaret followed Julia to the library, a room only slightly more satisfactory than the living room. The lowered shades made it dark and lonely. All of the dead Mr. Chalmers's books seemed to be in deluxe editions, and the backs of all of them were exactly in line on the shelf. The magazines were neatly arranged on a table. Not a broken binding. His desk was in perfect order, as he had left it, probably, the pen and pencils ready for use, an unopened paper on the fresh green blotter. Snapshots of Julia and Jack in silver frames stood behind the large brass inkwell. The mahogany wastepaper basket at the side was empty.

Julia brought a handsomely framed photograph of Mr. Chalmers, and Margaret heard herself make a ghastly remark, "What a marvelous watch chain!" She hastened to repair the damage. "A splendid man, Julia. No wonder you are proud of him." Julia rehearsed his death. It had been a most conventional death, embroidered with much sobbing and many farewell words. "And afterwards he looked so peaceful and happy," finished Julia, weeping behind her handkerchief.

"Oh, but dying takes such a minute, Julia. It's living that takes the time and the courage." She was thinking of Richard, but Julia misunderstood.

"I know. I want to die. I can't live like this. I can't, I can't." She was so pitiful that Margaret's irritation melted to tenderness.

"My dear, my dear, I know." They sat quietly for a time. "Julia, your hair is exactly the color of honey."

"He used to say that."

"Then you see it must be true." Julia smiled at last, tremulously. For a few minutes they were on common ground, very gentle with each other and friendly. Then it developed that Julia felt sorry, very sorry indeed, for Margaret.

"It's hard enough to have to bear one's loss without having to worry about—other things. I have thought about you often and wished it might have been different."

"You mean the lack of money?"

Julia nodded. "Of course I know Richard did the best he could. Four children cost a great deal—and your poor mother. I realize, perhaps more than you do, that Richard lacked confidence in his own powers. He was rather too easily discouraged. Something may have happened to shake his confidence; one can't tell."

A tempest of anger shook Margaret's breast. Patronizing Richard like that! Belittling him! Pitying him! As if she had broken his heart. It was unbearable.

"Oh, it wasn't like that at all," she cried. Julia was looking benevolent. It occurred to Margaret that she really thought she was being kind and generous. *It gives her a lot of pleasure.* Richard's words. And it didn't hurt them; it couldn't. They knew and they were perfectly secure. What Julia thought didn't alter the truth in the least. The tempest died down.

"You see we lived together so long . . . But don't feel sorry, Julia, about money. We don't have to worry, Richard took care of that, you know. We have what we want." She told about the three boarders and the column in Saturday's paper.

"You are very plucky," said Julia.

Margaret tapped her foot impatiently on the floor. I won't be called plucky, she wanted to shout. I won't. I won't.

Then she realized that Julia was about to say something important.

"My dear, when I went out to the cemetery last week I walked over to your lot. I had been thinking of you, and I wanted to see where Richard lay. Are you planning to put up a monument?"

"Why, no," said Margaret. A monument for Richard, who hated display and ceremony and doing conventional things?

"Then I want you to look at this." Julia unrolled a sheet of drawing paper and spread it out on the desk, weighing the corners to keep it flat. Margaret leaned over to look at it. A sketch of Mr. Chalmers's monument, was her first thought, then she noticed the inscription: "In Memoriam" above and, underneath, Richard's name, the date of Richard's birth, and the date of Richard's death.

"I went to the same sculptor who designed Mr. Chalmers's mausoleum," Julia was explaining. "He is considered very fine. Margaret dear, I want to do this for Richard, with your permission."

Margaret gripped the edge of the desk, and kept her eyes on the sketch, although she could scarcely see a line of it. Once she had seen a woman in hysterics. If I laugh or if I cry, either one, she thought, I'll be like her. I mustn't. I mustn't. Yet she wanted to so very much. She wanted to shout with laughter at the absurdity of Julia's erecting a monument to Richard—how amused he would be!—and she wanted to cry because she resented it. She could not give her consent; of course not.

She looked at Julia. The mask of grief had vanished, and instead she saw what was almost radiance. There was no doubt about it! Her face was tender and beautiful.

Line by line the drawing stood out from the blur before her eyes. The design, she realized, was symbolic: the hooded figure at the top was Death; the young man at his feet was Richard. And the work was really quite exquisite. Oh, Richard, what shall I do?

"Isn't it beautiful?" whispered Julia.

He'll understand. He always understands, Margaret said to herself. And to Julia, "It's a wonderful thing for you to do, Julia; of course I am willing."

Mary

Nineteen, almost twenty, Mary came home from school that June with a high heart. We who were older used to watch her as one watches a child learning to walk. We didn't want her to get a tumble. We wanted to let her down very gently into life.

Mary wasn't in the least afraid of life. She had a zest for it, a tremendous appetite that would swallow the bitter along with the sweet and content itself with a momentary grimace. Mary really believed you could take life that way—quaff your medicine and cry for more. Mary, to use her own phrase, was simply going to eat up life. Just as it came. No complaining, no regretting, no disillusioning. Mary, you see, trusted life. She frolicked on the knees of the gods.

She smiled on Jim and she smiled on Taylor, as she smiled on everyone else, because life was so much fun. She loved to jump out of bed at six, pull on her bathing suit, fly in the sedan along the road to the country club, only slowing down a little for the other girls as they came out. She loved to dive into that cool green water, to lose for a moment—but a moment only—her element of warmth and sunshine and breeze; the earth was so much the dearer when she came back to it. That was the way to begin a day! And she ended it, how? Oh, dancing, probably, her blood beating in time with the music, fast, throbbing, a little wild, oh, queer, maybe—as if she and Jim or Taylor (it made no difference) were one person instead of two, and hardly a person at that, but something very light and thin, beaten about by the pulse of the music, whirled faster, faster, faster, like that! Very queer, but any amount of fun.

Between the morning swim and the evening foxtrot, well, there was the sedan to carry the crowd around shopping—shopping is far from being a burden when one is twenty; and bridge and picnics in the wood; and, two mornings a week, the day nursery that some of them had organized for charity. The girls took turns with the babies. Mary adored it. She would, of course.

Not wholly selfish, you conclude? Well, when one is twenty and the world is good, one sees poverty and disaster and heartbreak from afar. Mary's eyes used to be warm, not with trouble, but with the thrill of rubbing shoulders with trouble. She used to put on her prettiest dresses when she went to the day nursery. "The poor little things," she would cry, hugging the prettiest baby. A sweet picture, and it may be Mary knew it; a tender madonna, dreamy-eyed.

There were other days when she drove out to the Old Ladies' Home. "Look what I brought you, dear—pansies! I picked them for you. And a red rose for Mrs. Watkins. Isn't it a beauty?" She used to kiss each one on the cheek. And it must have pleased her, I am sure, to see trembling old fingers reach out for a fold of her dress. She would bend down, sometimes, and lift their hands to her face and laugh, and wrinkle her nose with its wreath of impudent freckles.

She gave us pleasure. And pleasure was so easy to give, so pleasant to give. She had only to look up at Taylor in the appealing way that was as natural to her as breathing and his eyes would grow dark and tender, and she could tell by the way his lips tightened that she had stirred him. Taylor, mind you, ten years older than she, and a man of the world! Or with Jim—a smile not so appealing this time, jolly and companionable. And Jim's lower lip would quiver and, if he thought no one could see, he might touch his cheek to her arm, the barest touch, but enough to show that he cared more than one might think. She would laugh and push him away.

All summer they talked of the fall. Should it be school again for Mary? Or Europe? Or what? Mary decided for herself, in favor of a year at home. "Dad and Mother really need me, you know; I'm all they have." Almost a martyr, one might think. So her father ordered a new sedan, with her monogram painted on the door, and her mother took her to New York for a fortnight's shopping just as the theaters were opening, and she stopped to visit three different school friends on the way home, one of whom had married and actually given birth to a baby. Mary told us how she helped bathe it, and how she warmed its bottle of water, and learned to add a pinch of soda for the colic. Quite maternal and competent, looking ahead, perhaps, to another possible baby in the future and the young mother's role.

It was Thanksgiving before she came back, with a new squirrel coat which made her look fairer and pinker than ever. Jim and Taylor were both at the station, and she held out a hand to each simultaneously and called, "Bless your hearts, boys," like the friend she had visited at Yonkers, and rode home with Mother and Dad in the new sedan.

Only three weeks until Christmas, and such stacks of things to do! Especially nice gifts to be made for the girls she had just visited, and toys for the day nursery, and little satin bags and handkerchiefs for the old ladies. Also a beaded bag to be finished for Mother, and a quilted bathrobe to be chosen, very carefully, for Dad. She had brought me a blue glass bowl from Tiffany's, exquisitely fragile; ran in with it under her arm the day before Christmas on her way to trim the old ladies' tree. "Never was so busy, Auntie," she said. "It's the best Christmas ever!" And she buttoned up the squirrel collar and ran lightly out to the sedan, whose backseat was piled with white packages tied with red ribbon and adorned with sprigs of holly. She blew me a kiss as she turned the corner.

It was, of course, a busy time; boys and girls home from college, dancing every night, luncheon parties, skating, a dazzling time. Mary shining like a star, smiling on everyone, looking up soberly at Taylor, sticking out her tongue at Jim, always thinking up something new, always eager, always radiant.

She didn't have time for a single deep breath, she declared, until the boys and girls had gone back to school. And then it was winter, a glorious winter, with plenty of snow for skiing and snow-shoeing and sleigh riding. I used to walk out with them, sometimes, on moonlit nights and sit on a blanket in the snow to watch the fun. Mary had a red knitted suit that she had worn the year before at a Lake Placid house party, with a cocky little tam-o'-shanter to match, and she used to stand as straight as a young tree when she came flying down the ski slide and took the jump like a boy, arms wide, head up, a crimson cross against the snow. It made one glow to watch her. "Good one, Mary," Jim would shout, and I could hear the soft ripple of her laugh through the cold.

But there were times, I think, when she preferred Taylor. She liked to have him bring her a volume of Katherine Mansfield or Amy Lowell, that they might discuss it as equals, seriously, thoughtfully. Nothing too radical, of course, too . . . well, you know how careful Taylor would be. And they used to argue hotly about everything under the sun: socialism, death, Russia, friendship. Mary was almost her happiest in an argument; and it was especially nice to argue with Taylor because he never lost his balance. Mary did, sometimes; she was inclined to exaggerate, to make her points too strong, and when she did, Taylor could take her down without boasting or conceit, by a perfectly good-natured little quip of some sort that showed her just where she stood.

Sometimes Mary would play for him, sitting at the baby grand Dad had given her for Christmas . . . "On the Road to Mandalay" . . . very sweetly, looking up at Taylor as he leaned above her, looking down at the keys again, shyly, proudly.

Spring was so wet and miserable, and Dad's cough hung on so long that she took him to Los Angeles in March for a real vacation. "Dad needs it desperately," she told me, looking worried. "He has worked so hard all these years. He's such an old dear. I know it will do him worlds of good." It did, too. I don't think he ever spent a pleasanter time in his life than those six weeks of sitting on hotel verandas, watching Mary start off for the golf links in her new white flannel dress, or listening to the orchestra beating out impassioned music for Mary's feet, or lying in the sand while Mary frolicked in the white-crested surf. She had a charming way, he told me later, of scampering up the beach, all dripping, to kiss him and arrange his cushion under his head, before she scampered back to hurl her young body through the dark green waves as they broke.

"I'm so glad that I stayed home this year," she told me when she came back. "It's meant such a lot to Mother and Dad." It did. And to all of us. I am sure of it.

She had brought two friends from Denver home with her to be entertained with the usual orgy of bridge parties, golf, and dancing. They even had a masquerade, with the most elaborate of costumes. Mary was a canary, all in yellow feathers with a train like a tail, and when the masks were torn aside they made her climb into the orchestra balcony and sing, once, twice, three times. Then she balanced on the railing like a bird, and jumped so lightly that it seemed like flying to the floor, and to Jim—and whirled around and around with him while the violin took up the latest foxtrot.

It was nearly summer when they left, and Mary took her mother to Chicago for her summer wardrobe. Mother had always stinted herself so; she was so dear and unselfish. Mary had a heavenly time leading her from shop to shop, managing the whole outlay herself, deciding which gown to take (and it was seldom the cheapest), superintending the alterations, and insisting on the youngest hats. "No old lady in our family yet a while." And she ordered ten lovely shirts for Dad so that he wouldn't feel left out. And just to please Mother, Mary picked up a few things for herself, including an imported frock of white lace and pink chiffon to wear at Eloise and Bob's wedding. Mary was to be maid of honor, and Taylor was to be the best man.

There were festivities innumerable preceding that wedding, showers and dinners and bridal luncheons. "The sweetest wedding in the world," Mary told me, her eyes misty. "And, Auntie, they're going to live in that perfectly darling English cottage by the park. Eloise has the dearest kitchen, with ruffled curtains and a breakfast nook, all stenciled in blue . . ." That faraway look . . .

Everyone thought Mary lovelier than the bride, as she walked very, very slowly down the church aisle. And afterward, with Taylor, well, it set the town to wondering how long it would be before Taylor . . . or Jim . . . Mary, too, I think, was beginning to wonder. She seemed to become conscious, quite suddenly, of a treasure house to which she held the key, and her eyes were alight with anticipation. There seemed to be an actual cloud of glory about her as she walked . . . to me, at least.

I wonder why I wanted to hold her back, to keep her from choosing?

Well, Mary made her choice. And it came about in this fashion: she devised a test. How naively the young do these things, as if they were solving a problem in geometry, Q.E.D. at the end. It was like Mary to choose her birthday, and Rock Rapids, and it was like her to invite an audience, however unsuspecting, to witness the ordeal—three carloads, including Mother and Dad and Jim and Taylor and as many of the regular crowd as could get away. It was also like Mary to select a road few cars ever attempted. She loved to be jounced and tossed and shaken all about.

"Mary," begged her father, "have you no consideration for the car?"

"Not a bit, darling," she laughed. "When it goes to pieces, we can walk."

Taylor, sitting beside her, smiled as one smiles at a kitten chasing its tail.

Jim was waiting at the rapids, hands on his belt, feet apart, jealous no doubt of her company, but careful not to show it. Together they strolled to the water's edge. That is only one picture of a score I have kept in my heart to remember that day; Mary balancing on a fallen log, hand in hand with Jim . . . black water below, white water above . . . Mary sitting like a figurehead carved on the prow of a black rock . . . running like a sandpiper along the bank . . . stepping into a green canoe . . . running back, her bright hair tormented by the wind, to gather firewood and wrest the tablecloth from her mother's hands . . . inspired at the last minute to swim once around the pool before eating, dashing for the bathhouse with a red bathing suit under her arm . . . back again in a minute, little rivulets still dripping from her hair, her skin rubbed and rosy. Eating, as she insisted, like a starved whale. That is the way life was for Mary.

After lunch she lay down with me on my steamer rug, spread on the slippery pine needles, brown and sweet, not too far from the rapids, and she fell asleep with her cheek in one hand, like a month-old baby. No lover could have watched her more jealously than I. The other arm lay limp on the dark rug, the palm turned trustingly up. That seemed significant—and a little pathetic—to me, for I know how older people sleep, people who have seen trouble, with hands so tightly closed.

Presently she awoke, as quietly as she had fallen asleep. She lay for a time, braiding and unbraiding the fringes of the steamer rug. She was puckering her forehead, pulling the pencil-stroke curves of her eyebrows together as she wrestled with some problem of importance. We were always amused when Mary put her mind on anything, wrongly, no doubt; yet we loved her best when she didn't stop to think.

Mary sat up, shaking back the gold threads of her hair. She hugged her knees and looked at the rapids more wistfully than was usual for her.

"Do you know what Eloise told me the day before the wedding?" she began. "Why, she said she was afraid."

"Of what?"

"Everything under the sun. Afraid they'd have a baby that would die . . . afraid they wouldn't be happy . . . afraid she'd grow too fat, and she will if she doesn't take any exercise. But don't you think that's dreadful?"

"Do you think she was really afraid, or just admitting to herself that there are bad spots in a good life, Mary?"

Mary shrugged her shoulders. "I don't know, but I think it is perfectly terrible to start out like that. Bob isn't a bit that way. He just laughs at her. I wouldn't like that. I'd want my husband to feel exactly as I did about everything. It seems to me that ought to be the test: to have the same things bore you, and the same things thrill you. Don't you? As for being afraid . . . well, I'm not going to have bad spots in my good life, not at all."

You see what a child she was!

"Jim," she called. "Taylor." Taylor came first, as if he had waited a long time for that call. Jim sauntered after him, whistling at the treetops.

"Who wants to shoot the rapids with me?"

Now Mary knew those rapids as well as anybody, their treachery and their danger.

"Suicide, Mary." Taylor dismissed it like that.

Mary pouted. "The Indians do it; I've seen them."

"Indians, yes."

"Well, let's be Indians, then."

"You little daredevil!" Taylor was amused. He liked to think of her as a little daredevil, to be held back by his strong arms, I suppose.

"Then you won't go?"

"Neither will you, Mary; it's foolish, and you know it."

"Of course it's foolish." Mary was annoyed. "Don't you ever like to be foolish?"

"Not with you."

She studied him a moment with displeasure. Then, "Jim, will you?"

Jim, still whistling, walked over to the bank, and took his time about surveying the rapids, as though mapping in his mind the position of every rock and every twist of the channel.

"I'll say I will," he answered.

"But, Mary . . . ," I called after them. A silly picture I must have made, pursuing them up the slippery trail, as if an old woman could halt love in its course. I didn't follow far. For I saw Jim take her arm and rub his cheek against it; this time it was more than the barest touch, and I saw the sudden burning in Mary's cheek. I believe that passion leapt like a flame between them. And as they rounded the great rock above the rapids, I saw Mary's arms reaching up about his neck—no more, but I am sure that they clung there for a moment in close embrace, lip to lip. I turned back.

It was only a matter of seconds before the green canoe slid over the ridge at the top of the rapids. Jim was kneeling in the stern, bent low, his white shirt ballooning out over his shoulders. Mary knelt in the bow, holding her shining paddle high. No hint of fear in either face, only a sort of high intoxication as if they had just tasted some miraculous wine.

Out they shot, straight for the narrowing V that marked the channel. The bow tipped down. Jim leaned back, bending his body to hold them true. They swerved with precision between wet boulders. No Indian ever managed it more skillfully. Straight down they came, just grazing a submerged tree trunk near the bottom, evading the sucking whirlpool below, until the green shell floated motionless under the willows in the quiet water.

Safe, we said to ourselves. Safe!

That was Mary's test, and I am inclined to believe it was not such a bad test after all. It had not been mere folly, for Jim had brought them through it; it had proved more, I think, than Mary dreamed.

Taylor was the first to reach them. Mary put both of her hands around him and looked up with her old smile. She seemed puzzled, hurt a little, when he turned away. Without the faintest idea, you see, of how things were with him. Then someone honked from the waiting cars, and we all climbed in. Mary rode with Jim in his roadster, and you can guess as well as I of what they spoke as they sped home in the warm glad dusk.

Jim, we were told the next day, would wait six weeks and no

longer. "And why so long?" he wanted to know. Couldn't he understand all that had to be done? The dainty garments that had to be made with so much delight and packed away in drawers padded with sachet; the plans that had to be drawn for the little house Dad insisted on providing; the teas and luncheons and slumber parties, the invitations and announcements and lists; and at the last the flood of gifts that left bare the shelves of the jewelers and made quick profits for the furniture stores and gift shops and the dealers in fine china. When Mary's tremulous fingers mixed the cards and broke a sherbet glass into a thousand glittery pieces, we sent her away with Jim. It was the morning of their wedding day. Mary was wearing a rosy linen dress, I remember, and she looked like a very little girl as she and Jim swung hand in hand up the path that led to the clover field behind the house.

They were married in the garden, on a night made radiant by a full moon that was constant and a thousand Japanese lanterns that were as fickle as the breeze that swayed them. Where the first chrysanthemums nodded their shaggy heads, we had made an altar. The smell of clover blossoms and autumn roses mingled with the muted strains of the orchestra hidden behind the porch vines. The faint tinkle of dishes and silver floated from the teahouse. Bright frocks and soft voices were blown about like thistledown on the grass.

It must have been because Mary tried to be so solemn and dignified that she looked so eternally young, her cheeks so flushed, her eyes so brilliant, her hair such a mystic gold under the floating veil. Kisses for everyone, especially Taylor, and the biggest of all for Dad.

"This is only the very beginning of my life," Mary whispered to me when the time came for them to go.

Oh, I believed that life could do no less than send forth those two with her blessing. Jim, it seemed, made the wall of love that protected our Mary complete and high and safe from disaster . . .

Well, they did have a week of it, a week of bliss unmarred; but a week is a short season if it must enfold all one's youth.

Very likely I am making too much of what ended it. Death, I

remind myself, might have stood on the mountain road to strike them down, but forebore. And there are other catastrophes beyond a crippled body. Besides, the doctors are beginning to prophesy these last few days that Jim will walk again.

We heard of it, Mary's father and mother and I, in the garden where the happy ghosts of Mary's wedding were still playing. It was a telegram, we kept saying to ourselves, like any other telegram; on yellow paper, neatly typed . . . the accident that crippled Jim was like any other accident, an overturned car on a mountain road. Mary, we were told, was safe.

They meant her body, of course. They didn't understand that something exceedingly precious had perished in that instant's happening, nor did they see what was born in that same instant to replace it.

"She will be brave about this," said Mary's father.

Everyone agreed as to that. For it required courage to come back to the little house where they were to have been joyful, with Jim lying so still on a stretcher; and it required courage to face a new universe in which pain was master, and in which love was less a rapture than a servant to pain.

Mary came to me today. I was sitting in my bedroom window when I saw the sedan slow to a stop on my driveway. I wanted to see her jump out, as she used to, and dash across the grass to the steps. I wanted to hear the slamming of the screen door and the clear "Yoo-whoo!" drifting up from the hallway. But not today. She sat quite still in the car for a long time before she fumbled with the door catch, stepped down as laboriously as you or I, walked, oh so slowly, around the lawn on the hard white concrete walk, and closed the screen as quietly as though a baby were asleep just inside. I went down to greet her.

A little pale, our Mary, a little strained about the eyes and mouth. She pressed her face into a bowlful of asters, pink and blue and lavender and white, that stood on a table by my window; and she sighed, and smiled in apology for the sigh. When I sat down against the absurdly gay cretonne of my wicker chair, she stopped to arrange the footstool that I often like to use.

"Oh, Mary," I found myself saying, "don't think about me!"

Mary sat on the floor, leaning her head against my knee. The color poured into her face.

"No one ever told me," she cried, "how selfish I was! Oh, darling, the things I have learned!"

"Hard things," I said, for I cannot forgive life for hurting her.

"Oh, yes, but good things, too."

She told me about them. Even money, it developed, had become a problem, for they couldn't—surely I realized that they couldn't depend on Dad. Jim had a plan, in which she could help. They must, of course, live simply, sell Jim's roadster, save what they could for rainy days. Nothing mattered so long as she had Jim . . .

I could feel her body trembling against my knee as she spoke of Jim.

"I hear only good reports," I said to comfort her.

"If I only dared believe them," she whispered, as though the very thought might bring calamity.

Oh, don't you see what had happened to her? How life had failed its trust with her? Brave she was, yes, when I wanted her carefree; patient when I wanted her eager; good when I wanted her lovely.

While we were quiet, a car jogged past on the pavement, loaded to the running boards with brilliant sweaters and caps and pennants. There must have been a football game, for the streamers were trailing out behind, and the horn was doing its best to sing the appropriate air on its single key. Will you believe me when I tell you that Mary didn't see them at all, or hear that syncopated honking?

"It's worse at night," she said. "I know he's lying there in the dark with his jaw set, trying not to call me."

The Blue Spruce

Swan Swanson was rolling his thick red sweater over his hips when he saw Lars Olson drive past his house on his way to the ski tournament. Lars Olson was standing on the floor of his sleigh, with his feet far apart, and the reins loose in his hand. His long skis, propped against the driver's seat, were like yellow saplings against the sky. He wore his orange stocking cap with the tassel swinging by a twisted cord, and he also had on his great orange sweater, although Swan Swanson could only see the collar of it rising out of his fur coat. It was a coonskin coat, yellow and white and brown, and Lars Olson had bought it just a year ago with the prize money he had won at the tournament.

His horses flattened their ears and stretched their necks as his whip cracked with a sharp sound like river ice breaking in the spring, and they skimmed the road with their fat bellies. Their little harness bells jingled. Lars Olson slued past without once looking towards Swan Swanson's house, although it stood in its clearing only two rods from the road.

Swan Swanson laughed at that. He sat down on the log he had squared the winter before with his axe, close to the stove, and pulled his socks over his big feet—four pair of socks, diminishing in length from first to last, so that the tops of the exterior pair were four stripes under the knees of his red mackinaw trousers. He grunted as he tugged at his rubber pac boots. Then, standing up, he worked himself into his red mackinaw coat and pulled his red stocking cap well over his bulging ears and under his sweater collar at the back, so that nothing of him could be seen except his blue eyes and his little pink nose and his yellow mustache. Finally he took his double-yarn mittens from the shelf and his skis from the corner by the door, and stepped out into the snow.

The day was cold and clear and perfectly silent. There were no clouds to drop fresh snow on the ski slide, no hazy thaw to melt its hard-packed surface. The very air seemed frozen. It pricked Swan Swanson's nostrils, as he bent over his skis, so that big drops gathered on the tip of his nose. It drew tears to his eyes, and it rang in his ears like a hundred clanging bells. He stamped his skis on the snow. Yesterday the sun had been warm enough to melt the surface the least little bit, and the night had refrozen it in a thin, glassy sheet, slightly pebbled, which cracked and crumbled under the skis, and exposed the snow underneath, loose and light and granular, like sugar.

He plunged his pole in the snow, and pushed himself forward. The red-tipped points of his skis, upturned, ran ahead of him between the trees. His pole made deep, slanting holes in the drifts. He crossed the old logging road down which Lars Olson had driven, and struck out, across country, through the burned timber. All around him were the silver corpses of pine trees killed by the forest fires. They looked like gigantic steel pins stuck in a white cushion. Sometimes Swan Swanson had to duck under a corpse which had fallen and been caught in the arms of its dead neighbor; sometimes he had to vault, skis swinging awkwardly, over a protruding limb or a barbed-wire fence; sometimes he climbed a hill with staggered skis pointing outward; sometimes he had to turn sidewise and cut steps for himself in the steep side of a snowbank. When he could, he coasted; when he couldn't, he glided, and he could stop himself almost instantly by a little jump and a swing to either side.

II

Swan Swanson came, after a while, to the top of a hill, and he halted for a minute and looked down, because he could see from there, as from nowhere else within miles, the broad, cold surface of Lake Superior. Today it was on fire with the cold. The steam was rolling up from it like smoke. The white ice rimmed the shore. Streaks of white floated on the blue. Swan Swanson laughed. He liked the cold. The tighter the mercury hugged itself in the bulb of his thermometer, the louder he laughed.

Between him and the lake lay the town, through which he had to pass on his way to the tournament. From above it was a great white field, broken only by the stovepipes and black smoke which rose like pillars, straight up to the sky. Swan Swanson yelped, and lunged forward, and swooped down upon the town like a hawk.

Usually the town, in winter, was buried and silent. Only an occasional load of logs, or a boy with a muffler and a sled, or a woman wrapped in shawls and bending to meet the wind could be seen. And the houses, on ordinary days, were like toys lost in the snow, buttressed, as they were, with the drifts, halfway to the tops of the windows, capped with snow on their roofs, and cut off from the sun by the thick frost which lined their windows.

But today was tournament day, and the snow had been shoveled away from the doorways, and the yellow pine doors in the storm sheds of the Bee Hive Store and the barbershop and the Svenska Café banged pleasantly as the lumberjacks and farmers and timber cruisers marched in and out. In front of the post office sleighs were waiting, while their drivers stamped their feet and flapped their arms and blew their noses with their fingers into the drifts. Swedes and Norwegians and Finns, laughing and jabbering, were crowding into the sleighs and digging their feet into the straw which lay in the bottom, and drawing the quilts on which they sat over their shoulders, and tucking the bearskin robes under their knees. These were mostly the women and children and old folks. The men preferred their skis. A few even preferred to tramp laboriously on snowshoes. The snow was etched with the long double grooves of the ski tracks and the crisscross of the webbing of the snowshoes.

At the Grand Hotel, Swan Swanson, who was gliding through the smooth snow at the roadside, passed Lars Olson's sleigh. His horses were pawing and whinnying and jangling their bells, and sweating steam all over their bodies. They had frost on their flanks and icicles on their chins and red paper rosettes on their harnesses. Swan Swanson shook his fist at them and laughed. For Lars Olson was boasting, no doubt, by the red-hot stove in the hotel, and flapping the skirt of his coonskin coat, and telling how Swan Swanson, in the tournament last year, had landed on a little blue spruce tree and had rolled heels over head down the hillside. Swan Swanson, he would say, guffawing, whose two first jumps had been longer than anyone else's, had been so sure he would win with the third . . . and instead, he had rolled heels over head down the hill. Ha! Ha! Ha! And Lars Olson, who had jumped almost as far, and had landed on his feet, had won, and had bought his coonskin coat. Ha! Ha! Ha!

Laughing, Swan Swanson left the road at the edge of town, and struck out, once more, through the woods. Not dead woods, this time, but second growth, green and brown and sappy. The spruce and firs were squatting in the snow, touching the top of it with their lowest branches. The pines, jack and white and Norway, held the skirts of their boughs much higher, and some of them were humped about the shoulders, like women wading in a river, looking down solicitously at their long, rough legs. Around the base of every tree was a depression, where the heat of the living wood had melted the snow, and the shadows, there and everywhere, were lavender. Where there were no shadows, there was the bleak, bluish waste of snow, which glinted with tiny points of red and violet and yellow. The patches of glare ice on the frozen streams, across which Swan Swanson leaped on his skis, were as blue as the sky.

Yelping and grimacing and singing, he climbed three hills and coasted into three valleys. He unbuttoned his mackinaw, and pulled the mittens from his big red hands. His white breath was hot on his chin. He stretched out his collar to cool his sweating neck. At the top of the fourth hill he swerved back to the road, because he could see ahead of him the wooden scaffolding, yellow with the sun shining on it, and the ski slide, like a long white scroll on the next and highest hill. The clubhouse lay buried at its foot . . . a few tiers of logs and a smoking stovepipe in the snow. Everywhere the people stood in groups, like patterns of bright color on a screen. And as he stooped for his final coast, he heard, behind him in the road, the little jingling bells of Lars Olson's team, and saw the tassel of his orange cap rise over the crest of the hill. Swan Swanson wrinkled his face in a laugh.

III

Swan Swanson drew the first place. There were thirty-three of them, stamping and laughing, and joking. He fastened his number to the chest of his red sweater, and threw down his mackinaw coat and his double-yarn mittens. He flapped his arms and stamped his feet and climbed the ladder which rose from the hilltop to the peak of the slide. The country below him was as white and as smooth as a frosted cake, and the evergreens were like candles, ready for the match.

Swan Swanson stood on the platform at the top, and shoved his toes into the straps of his skis and slipped the thong well over his heel. The wooden slide, padded with evergreen boughs and covered with a layer of snow, packed and firm, was a precipice at his feet. In a minute now, Swan Swanson would slide down that sheer descent to the takeoff halfway down the hill, and he would shoot out into space from that takeoff like a ball from a cannon, and if he were lucky, he would land on his feet somewhere near the blue spruce which was planted like a warning in the snow. Swan Swanson felt the muscles ripple in his legs and arms and torso. He laughed.

There he stood at the top with his great arms folded on his chest. There was a bugle call. He heard its echoes in the valley. Then he crouched and glided forward and plunged down the steep and slippery slide. The air was a whistle in his ears. The trees were a streak before his eyes.

71

He straightened when he reached the takeoff. He flung out his arms like wings, and like wings they bore him through the air. He seemed to be soaring over the tops of the little firs. The wind was a hurricane on his face and chest. He looked for the little blue spruce, and he saw it, at last, far ahead, on his left. If he had been a hawk, he could have reached it with two flaps of his wings. If the slide had been steeper . . . if his start had been faster . . . But the ground was eager for his feet; it drew him down like a magnet. The little blue spruce was still three yards ahead of him when he landed with a tremendous whack in the snow. Yelping, he coasted triumphantly to the bottom of the hill, and waved his arms, and laughed at the crowd.

Swan Swanson did not immediately climb back to the hilltop. Instead he stood as near as he dared to the little blue spruce. He stripped a handful of its juicy needles and chewed them as he waited. His eyes narrowed to a little slit when he saw an orange sweater and an orange cap on the top of the slide. Lars Olson, who had been first last year, was now twenty-first. He was a Baltimore oriole with long, yellow toes. Yet he crouched like a cat, and like a cat he jumped, claws spread, and like a cat he landed on his feet not two yards behind the blue spruce. He grinned at Swan Swanson as he passed.

Swan Swanson snapped a bough from the tree. He stuck a piece of it through the stitches of his sweater. He glared and frowned and spat in the snow and mumbled in Swedish as he climbed with his long skis over his shoulder past the crowd to the top of the hill.

The bugle notes, this second time, were clear and true and very cold. Swan Swanson crouched even lower than Lars Olson; he leaped even higher; he landed within four feet of the blue spruce. His laugh echoed in the valley as he veered to the left at the bottom of the hill.

A second time Swan Swanson waited by the blue spruce until he saw the orange streak of Lars Olson's body on the sky. He saw the grooves in the underside of Lars Olson's skis. Lars Olson seemed to keep himself aloft with the flapping of his long orange arms. He seemed to draw his knees up, so that his skis cleared the snow.

While he floated and soared, Swan Swanson chewed the ends of his yellow mustache.

The skis whacked on the snow. If Lars Olson had been ten feet to the left, he would have landed on the blue spruce. As it was, his second jump exceeded Swan Swanson's by more than a yard . . . provided, of course, he could keep his balance. Otherwise, Swan Swanson knew, as he bent to watch, that Olson might as well not have jumped at all.

Lars Olson struggled to right himself. He twisted and wiggled and pawed the air. He snorted and sputtered. He swore. He lurched, and caught himself; lurched again, and caught himself . . . and he toppled, at last, still struggling, into a drift. He rolled over down the bank. His skis spun like pinwheels on the Fourth of July.

Swan Swanson laughed until he doubled up. He thumped his knees and his broad red chest. He danced in the snow. He shook the snow from the boughs of the little blue spruce. Like a giant, now, he strode up the snowbanks. His hearty laugh bounded down the hillside. His long skis were like feathers on his wide shoulder.

He could now hardly wait for the bugle call. He looked, as he hurtled down, for the green-blue cone of the spruce. He flapped his great red arms and drew up his long yellow feet. And he saw, as he soared, the tip of the blue spruce under his hand.

He was jolted by the shock of his landing. The red tips of his skis tried to meet and cross and throw him to the ground. He struggled to hold them straight. He doubled up and twisted halfway around and pawed the air. He grunted and moaned and swore. He lurched, and caught himself; and lurched again, and caught himself again. He had no idea where he was, or how much farther he had to go, when he heard the cheers of the crowd. They were shouting: "Swan! Swan! Hi, Swan!" Still gesticulating like a clown, Swan Swanson swerved into a snowbank at the foot of the hill, and stood upright, with his arms outspread. He laughed, because around the corner of the log house, he saw Lars Olson hitching his team to his sleigh.

Swan Swanson, heavy with doughnuts and coffee and little Swedish cakes, set out for home on his red-tipped skis. He could feel the weight of the gold pieces in his mackinaw pocket. He chose the road because of the crowd. He pulled his cap over his eyebrows and rolled his sweater collar up to his mustache. Every time a sleigh passed him with jingling bells and laughter and singing, he yelped and waved his thick arm. It was dark. The sun had gone down under the snow at the edge of the sky. The lavender shadows had deepened to purple, and the white snow was a luminous gray. A little moon rolled like a wheel of ice along the treetops whose shadows ribbed the road.

Swan Swanson cleared his throat. Lustily he sang, as the sleighs slued past him: "Måndagen är en frivillig dag." His yodel echoed from a hundred snowy hills.

Black Child

Mama's Papa

Callie was sitting in the doorway, her bare toes curled over the splintered gray edge of the step, with Beatrice squirming in her arms.

"Callie," Mama had said, "you watch Washington and Leroy and Beatrice while I stir up the corn bread. And mind you don't wake your papa."

"Well'm."

Callie could hear Papa snoring on the bed, and the thud of Mama's spoon against the bowl. In the reddish dirt outside, Washington and Leroy were playing, pulling nails with Papa's hammer from a board they had found in the city dump down the road. Beatrice was crying for the nails.

"You shut up," said Callie, holding her more tightly.

She realized too late that she shouldn't have spoken. Washington had forgotten she was there. Now he said, "Callie, I's goin' to drive this nail in your toe!"

"No you ain't!"

"Sure am!"

Leroy rolled in the dust and grinned at Washington. "Go do it, Washington."

"If you does," warned Callie, "I tells Mama."

Washington was grinning and making faces as he picked up the hammer and the longest, sharpest nail. "Here I goes, Callie!"

Callie held her breath and clutched Beatrice and shut her

eyes. And then, suddenly, unexpectedly, she heard Washington say "Huh!" in his throat.

Callie looked where he was looking. Up the road, past the piles of broken crates and tin cans on the dump, around the gray board wall of the Texas Barbecue, bounded Mis' Carpenter's car. The sun was so bright on its windshield that it almost made Callie blind. Mis' Carpenter's car dipped in the holes and rose on the bumps, and presently it groaned and stopped in front of the house.

Mis' Carpenter leaned over the wheel and honked. Callie could see her long pink arms and the blue embroidery on her white dress and the diamonds on her finger.

Mama came out, scuffing along in her house slippers. "Good morning, Mis' Carpenter."

"Pearl," said Mis' Carpenter, leaning back and lifting one knee over the other so that Callie could see the shimmer of her white silk stocking, "Pearl, you've got to help me out." Mis' Carpenter threw out her hands and let them drop in her lap. "I can't get any decent help. That cousin of yours—what's her name? Bertha?—isn't any good at all. I have to watch her every minute, Pearl."

"Yes'm."

"You've simply got to help me out," Mis' Carpenter went on. "There are ten people coming for lunch tomorrow, Pearl, and I don't see how I can manage."

"Yes'm," said Mama, shoving Leroy away from the running board. "That means a lot of work, Mis' Carpenter."

"That's why you've got to help me," said Mis' Carpenter.

Mama didn't say anything for a minute. She looked around at Callie, trying to hang on to Beatrice, and at Washington staring at Mis' Carpenter with his mouth open, and at Leroy, playing with his toes.

"Mis' Carpenter," said Mama, rubbing her eyes with her knuckle, "I haven't nobody but Callie to leave with the children."

"Can't you get your cousin Bertha?"

"No, ma'am, I wouldn't like to ask Cousin Bertha."

"Well, leave them with Callie, then. I tell you, Pearl, I simply *have* to have you."

"Callie's only five, Mis' Carpenter."

Mis' Carpenter leaned over and smiled at Callie. "Aren't you big enough to look after the others, Callie? Just for one day?"

"Yes'm," said Callie, trembling a little.

"You see, Pearl," said Mis' Carpenter.

"Well'm, I'll try," said Mama at last, kicking the dust with the toe of her house slipper.

Callie knew that Mama was in a hurry to get back to the corn bread. If Papa woke up and the corn bread wasn't ready, he would sure be mad. But Mis' Carpenter wanted to talk.

"Pearl, you're the only colored woman I ever had who worked like a white woman."

"Yes'm."

Just then Washington went around to the back of Mis' Carpenter's car and made a little scratch with the nail he had pulled out of the board.

"Hst!" warned Callie. Washington stuck out his tongue.

Callie had missed what Mis' Carpenter said, but she could hear Mama. "Well, I don't rightly know as to that, Mis' Carpenter. I couldn't say. I've wondered myself sometimes."

"You're so very light, Pearl. Is your mother light?"

"No, ma'am, Mama's as dark as Callie, but Papa was bright."

"Hm."

"Papa's mama was a widow woman, that's what he always said, Mis' Carpenter."

"I see."

"And when we asked him who was his papa, he used to get up and walk around and blow out his cheeks. 'My papa's name was John Webster Parsons.' That's all he ever said, Mis' Carpenter, and I was scared to ask him."

"There used to be a white family named Parsons around here," said Mis' Carpenter.

"Yes'm, I know that."

"Hm," said Mis' Carpenter.

Neither Mis' Carpenter nor Mama saw what Washington was going to do. Washington was going to drive a nail into Mis' Carpenter's tire. He winked at Leroy.

"Washington," said Callie in a whisper, "you quit that or I tells Mama."

Washington made a face at Leroy, and Leroy made a face at Callie.

Washington lifted the hammer to drive his nail.

"Mama!" called Callie.

Washington yelled all the time Mama was whipping him.

"That's what you get," said Mama. "Now you do like Callie says, and keep your hands off things that ain't yours."

"All right! Let me go!"

After Mis' Carpenter had driven away and Mama had gone back to the kitchen, Washington rolled for a long time in the dust, bawling and making faces. Leroy bawled too, and pounded his knees and looked at Callie as if he hated her. "Shut up, Leroy," warned Callie. She was scared. Suppose they woke Papa! Suppose Papa came out and whipped all of them!

Beatrice looked as if she were going to sleep. She made a bubble with her lips and sucked it in. Her eyes were little slits.

"Sh!"

Callie didn't see Washington until too late . . . until she saw his hand sneak up toward her from the ground, like the brown head of a snake. She tried to dodge, but Beatrice was too heavy on her knees. Washington took hold of Callie's bare leg with his fingernails. Callie saw him clench his teeth as he dug into her.

Callie made a hissing sound: "Jesus!"

"Mama," yelled Washington, triumphantly, "Callie's done said a bad word!"

II

The Baptizing

When Callie was seven, Mama went to cook for Mis' Carpenter.

"You have to do the best you can, Callie," said Mama. "And don't you let Beatrice out of your sight."

"Well'm."

"And if I'm late getting home, you'll have to give the baby some milk from the can."

"Well'm."

"I don't know what you're going to do about Washington."

"No, ma'am."

"And if your papa comes home, be sure you get him some dinner, Callie."

"Well'm."

Papa was working this summer, except when he was tired and had to lie in bed. He kept Mis' Carpenter's lawn, and Mis' Carpenter let him borrow the mower and rake and hoe and canvas basket that caught the grass so that he could keep other people's lawns as well. Once Callie had seen him standing in front of the Texas Barbecue, with the mower, and the tools tied on the handle. He had been talking to Mama's Cousin Bertha, spitting and kicking the dirt, and laughing all over.

"Colored men is triflin'," Mama used to say.

"That's Washington, too," thought Callie. "Triflin'!"

Today was Monday, and Mama had rubbed out the clothes before she went to get breakfast for Mis' Carpenter. "All you have to do, Callie," she said, "is rinse them and hang them out, but mind you do it right. I don't want no yellow clothes on my line."

"No, ma'am."

Usually, on washdays, Washington was bad. When Callie stood on the box to reach the clothesline, he would jerk it out from under her. Or he would run off with the clothespins. Once he told Leroy to throw dirt on the clean clothes, but Mama whipped him and he was scared to do it again. Sometimes Beatrice made trouble, and Callie would have to shake her and say, "Quit that or I tells Mama."

But today they were good. Washington didn't do a thing all the time Callie was rinsing and hanging out except sit on the step and look away off and whistle. And Leroy didn't do a thing except watch Washington's mouth and try to whistle himself. Beatrice sat on the ground and put dirt into a tin can. And the baby slept on the bed.

Callie was feeling happy, and Washington said, "Let's have a baptizing, what you say, Callie?" She said, "Huh! who you a-goin' to baptize, Washington?"

"Leroy," said Washington. "I's goin' to baptize Leroy."

"Where you goin' to baptize Leroy?"

"Where you s'pose?"

Callie knew what he meant. He meant the tank, and she was scared. The tank was down the road by the city dump. By the end of the summer it would be nothing but a big hole with tin cans in it, but now it was full of water which had run down from the dump when it rained. "Callie," Mama had said lots of times, "don't you forget that tank. If one of you was to fall in, you'd like to get drowned." And she used to add, sometimes, "Suppose one of the children fell in the tank, what would you do? Tell Mama."

Callie knew. "Roll 'em on a barrel, ma'am."

"Don't you forget now, Callie."

"No, ma'am. I won't forget."

So Callie was scared about the baptizing.

"Mama said we wasn't to go down by the tank, Washington."

"Going anyhow."

"No you ain't."

"Am!"

Washington started off down the road, kicking up the dust like smoke. Leroy ran after him. "Leroy," shouted Callie, clutching

Theodore and holding Beatrice by the hand. "You come back!"

But Leroy only ran the faster, and Callie had to go after them, dragging Beatrice down the road.

When she reached the tank, the baptizing had begun. Leroy was kneeling down and Washington was praying. "Brothers and sisters . . ."

"Washington," cried Callie. "Don't you dast!"

Washington showed his teeth. "Sister Callie, you shut your mouth!"

In spite of herself Callie snickered. She found an old bucket in the dump and sat down on it with Theodore.

"Brothers and sisters, let us pray."

Washington was praying just like the preacher. "We thank Thee, O God, for this here sinner come to repentance." Washington was waving his arms and rolling his eyes. "In the name of the Father . . ."

Callie lifted her head just in time to see Leroy go down into the tank, and come up again, choking and kicking.

"And of the Son . . ."

Callie was too scared to holler, for Leroy was limp when he came up the second time.

"And of the Holy Ghost . . ."

Callie grabbed Leroy by the leg just as Washington was about to duck him the third time. She hung on tightly. "Washington, you done drowned him!"

"Huh!" said Washington. Suddenly he looked scared and ran away up the road. Beatrice began to cry.

"Shut up," said Callie. "I've got to find me a barrel. Leroy, he's drowned." She laid the baby carefully on the ground.

Leroy was moaning and gulping in the mud. Callie began to pray as she hunted for a barrel. "O Jesus . . . O Jesus!"

Just a little way up the slope Callie found a barrel full of tin cans and broken bottles, and dragged it down to the tank. "Beatrice, you keep out of here." Heaving and tugging and pulling, she got

Leroy over the barrel. "Beatrice, if you touches that baby, I blisters you good."

Leroy was sick. He choked and cried in the mud. Callie rolled and rolled and rolled him on the barrel.

"Leroy, is you drowned?"

"I sure is!"

"You ain't dead yet, Leroy!"

Yet all the way home Callie was scared. Suppose Leroy fell down dead in the road . . . drowned! Suppose she hadn't rolled him long enough on the barrel!

They found Washington lying on the bed.

"If you tells Mama," he said hoarsely, opening one eye, "I calls the Law."

"I ain't a-goin' to tell nobody," said Callie, as she stripped off Leroy's overalls.

III

The Little Pin

Callie was helping Mis' Carpenter while Mama was in bed with the new baby.

"How are you going to manage about your work, Pearl?" Mis' Carpenter had asked.

"Mis' Carpenter," Mama had answered, "if you can get along without a cook for a week, I'll get my Cousin Bertha to wash, and Callie can do the ironing and the dishes and the cleaning. I've learned her how to work."

"But she's only eight," said Mis' Carpenter.

"Yes'm, but she knows how to work."

Today was Monday and Cousin Bertha had come to wash. Cousin Bertha was short and plump, and she wore black satin shoes with high heels and a red and yellow ensemble suit and a white lace hat, and she carried a red and purple bead bag over her arm.

"Now, Callie," said Cousin Bertha as she took off her suit coat in the washhouse, "you run in and ask Mis' Carpenter for a hanger for my coat, and then you can help me fill the boiler. I got a stitch in my side today."

While Callie lugged water from the hydrant in a bucket, Cousin Bertha peeled off her dress and put on her apron over her pink silk bloomers. Then she kicked off her shoes and stretched her toes and stuck them into her purple house shoes. Then she ran a string through her diamond ring and tied a knot in it and slipped it carefully over her hair, so as not to disturb her marcel.

"Now," said Cousin Bertha, "you can fill the tubs." And presently, "Callie, you rub out the white things while I goes in and makes me some ice water."

While she was gone, Callie found the little pin.

She had fished in the soapsuds until she brought up one of Mis' Carpenter's nightgowns with a lace yoke. Callie soaped it and rubbed it on the brass ridges of the washboard. It made a little clicking sound . . . once . . . twice. Callie wiped the sweat from her face and peered through the steam.

It was a little brass pin that fastened like a safety pin. Mis' Carpenter kept a card of them on her chiffonier. Callie disentangled it from the lace. "I'll give it to Mis' Carpenter when I goes in," she thought as she pinned it under the belt of her dress.

Callie never knew quite why she didn't give it to Mis' Carpenter. She thought afterwards that the devil must have got into her and made her envy Cousin Bertha's diamond, which swung between her breasts as she bent over the tub.

"I's going to have a diamond bar pin for my birthday," said Cousin Bertha. "But don't you tell nobody, Callie."

"Well'm."

"And my husband's going to rent the flat over the Texas Barbecue. Three rooms, Callie."

"Yes'm."

"Now you rinse the white things, Callie. I got to sit down and rest a bit." Cousin Bertha yawned. "I never got to bed till two last night and I'm that tired I'm like to die."

"Yes'm."

By the time the clothes were on the line and the tubs were emptied, it was noon, and Callie went into the kitchen to help Mis' Carpenter with lunch. "I'll give it to her just before I goes," thought Callie, feeling secretly for the hard back of the little pin under her belt.

She was chopping ice for the ice water when Cousin Bertha came to the door in her ensemble suit and her lace hat.

"Where's Mis' Carpenter?"

"Mis' Carpenter's talking on the telephone."

Cousin Bertha opened the icebox and took three eggs from the bowl on the shelf. Winking at Callie, she put them very carefully into the beaded bag on her arm, tiptoed across the back porch, down the steps, and out of sight beyond the gate.

Mis' Carpenter was smiling when she came back from the telephone. "You're a good girl, Callie."

"Yes'm," said Callie, holding her hand, like a little bowl, over the pin.

Callie walked home, after lunch, with the pin shining on the front of her dress, where it would show. "Just for tonight," she thought. She meant it, too. Tomorrow, when she was ironing, she would tell Mis' Carpenter she had found it in the gown. "You're a good girl, Callie," Mis' Carpenter would say.

Afterwards she wondered how she could have forgotten Mama. She might have known Mama would notice it the very first thing.

"Callie," called Mama from the bed where she was nursing the new baby. "You come here to me. Where you get that pin?"

"Found it."

"Where you find it?"

"In Mis' Carpenter's gown."

Mama sat up, and all the children formed a line, staring at Callie—Washington and Leroy and Beatrice and Theodore. Washington was grinning and rubbing his stomach.

84

"Callie, you done stole that pin."

Callie didn't want to answer, but she said at last, very low, "Yes'm."

For a minute nobody said anything. Then Mama got out of bed and put on her clothes. Callie didn't dare ask her what she was going to do. She didn't even dare look at Mama.

"You all come with me," said Mama, picking up the new baby.

Because Theodore couldn't keep up with them, Callie had to carry him on her hip. She dragged Beatrice along by the hand. Washington and Leroy ran along through the dust at the side of the road, making faces and teasing. "Mama's goin' take you to jail! Callie's a bad one! Callie's done stole Mis' Carpenter's pin!"

But Mama went straight up the road. Once she stopped in a vacant lot and sat down on the edge of the sidewalk to rest. Then she got up again and went resolutely on.

Callie knew where she was going. She was going to Mis' Carpenter's.

"Why, Pearl!" said Mis' Carpenter, at the kitchen door.

"Mis' Carpenter!" Mama was that tired she could hardly speak. "Callie's done stole your pin. Give it to her, Callie."

Hiding her face in Mama's skirt, Callie held out the pin.

"Oh, that!" laughed Mis' Carpenter. "It's nothing I want, Pearl. Let the child keep it."

"No, ma'am," said Mama. "She can't keep it."

"She's been a good girl, Pearl."

"I'm ashamed of Callie," said Mama.

All the way home Callie held her head very low.

"Callie," whispered Washington in her ear, "I'm goin' tell the Law!"

"No you ain't."

"He'll take you off in the hoodlum wagon, sure nuff."

"No he won't neither."

When they passed the Law in his blue uniform, swinging his

stick in front of the Barbecue, Callie was shaking from head to foot.

"Hello there," said the Law.

Callie put her arm over her face.

IV

The Law

Mama was sick. "Seems like I can hardly drag myself around," she told Cousin Bertha. "And how I'm going to manage with seven of them is more'n I know."

"What you ought to do, Pearl," said Cousin Bertha, "is send the kids to your mama. That's what I done with mine."

"I'd be awful lonesome, Cousin Bertha."

"I ain't lonesome," Cousin Bertha laughed, and she unwrapped the bundle she had brought under her arm. "I've got me a new red dress to wear to the dance."

"Where you get that dress?"

"Mis' Trasker gave it to me. I washed for her last week."

"That's a mighty nice dress to give away, Cousin Bertha."

Cousin Bertha grinned and winked at Callie.

The next morning Mama was sick so she could hardly get into her clothes. "I'd ask Cousin Bertha to help me out," she said as she braided her pigtails, "only Mis' Carpenter don't like her. I don't know what's got into Cousin Bertha."

Mama went very slowly up the road, waddling a little because she couldn't rightly see where she was going. Pretty soon Papa got up for breakfast, and after he had gone Callie cleaned house.

The baby was sleeping on the bed, with his legs drawn up to his stomach. Theodore and Beatrice were digging holes in the dirt by the step. Washington and Leroy had gone off somewhere.

Callie swept as well as she could with the old broom Mis' Carpenter had given Mama. Without disturbing the baby she straightened the sheet on the bed and the calico curtain that hung on a string over Papa's overcoat in the corner. She blew the dust from the vaseline bottle and the comb on the trunk, and from Papa's banjo. Then she went outside to the hydrant to draw the water for the mop.

While she was standing there, letting it run into the bucket, and thinking about Cousin Bertha's red dress, she saw the hoodlum wagon come down the road, jangling its bell. Callie was scared when it stopped on the corner by the Barbecue. She called, "Leroy! . . . Washington!"

Everybody was running towards the Barbecue. Terrified, Callie watched them pass, until, through the clouds of dust stirred up by their passing, she saw Washington plunging towards her, and after him Leroy. Washington was too scared to talk. He rolled his eyes, went into the house, and crawled under the bed.

Callie dragged the other children inside and shut the door.

"Leroy, what's matter?"

Leroy gulped with fright as he told her. "Cousin Bertha she done stole a dress from Mis' Trasker! A red silk dress!"

Callie bolted the door and barricaded it with the trunk. With trembling fingers, she let the window down, and pulled the shade to the bottom of the glass. Then she picked up the baby, and holding him very tightly, she sat down in the rocking chair so close to the window that she could peek under the corner of the shade. "If you hollers," said Callie to the children, in a whisper, "the Law'll git you!" After that they hardly dared to whisper. Leroy slid under the bed with Washington. Beatrice and Theodore stood close to Callie, clutching her dress.

Callie was never so scared in all her life as when she saw, under the curled edge of the shade, the Law marching up the road. He turned in front of the house and came straight into the yard.

"We got to git!" hissed Callie. "If you makes any noise, I busts you."

With the baby still in her arms, Callie lay down on the floor and wiggled under the bed. Beatrice and Theodore, fighting each other, crawled in after her.

They heard the Law pounding on the door. "Hey you kids, let me in."

"Sh!" warned Callie. She was so scared she felt sick. The baby started to cry, and she had to stuff her apron into his mouth.

"Callie!" hollered the Law. "Let us in! We won't hurt you. Honest we won't."

"Sh!" said Callie.

The Law was trying to break down the door . . . throwing himself against it. "They're kinfolk," she heard him say. "Maybe she run over here."

There was a creaking, a ripping, a rattling. The bolt gave way. The trunk crashed against the bed. Theodore screamed and Callie almost had to choke him to make him stop. "They'll git you, Theodore!"

In another minute the Law had seen them. "You little fools," he said, as he jerked them out, Theodore by the leg, Beatrice by the arm. Callie crawled out by herself, shielding the baby as best she could. The Law hauled Washington out by the seat of the pants. Washington kicked; the Law slapped him.

Callie couldn't stand that. She would have died first. As quick as lightning she put the baby on the bed and began fighting the Law—biting him, scratching his face, kicking his stomach. She had him wheezing and choking and striking out blindly. "You little hellcat," he said, getting hold of her hands and nearly twisting her arms off. "You fighting little hellcat!" He held her down in the rocking chair. "Where's Bertha? Tell me, and I'll let you go."

Callie was too scared to speak. Besides, the baby was yelling and she was afraid he would throw himself off the bed. Out of the corner of her eye she could see him lifting himself on his heels and his head, moving inch by inch toward the edge. Once a long time ago Beatrice had fallen off and cut her head on the rocker.

Just as Callie was bracing herself for the final struggle, she heard voices outside. "Sure they found her . . . right in the barbershop. Yes, sir."

88

The Law pushed Callie away from him. "You damn little fool!" he said. "Why didn't you tell me in the first place she wasn't here, eh?"

Callie, free at last, dived forward, and caught the baby just as he wiggled off the edge of the bed.

Fools

The news of the bank's failure fell upon Kate, like all the other thunderbolts which had tried in their time to wreck her, from a clear sky. She had never been more content with life. She did not mind in the least lying half paralyzed in her bed as she had been lying for the last five months, because she was sure of the future, Pauline's future. Kate was proud of what she had done for her daughter. She had earned and saved and salted away in Ben Hale's bank enough money to keep Pauline for the rest of her life, so that Pauline had now only to choose between her two suitors and the rest would be easy. Pauline would never have to wash or iron or chop cotton or wait on anyone's table, even her own. She would marry in all probability either Hoke Weatherby, with whom she had gone out an hour before to dance at the country club, or Ben Hale's son Harry.

Kate was amusing herself by wondering which one Pauline would choose when she heard the newsboy calling an extra. Quite plainly she could make out the word "bank" and the name "Hale," and because their combination on an extra spelled disaster for her she sent the nurse to get a copy.

Kate tried to read the headlines herself but her eyes failed her. They had not been good for much since her stroke. So she had to lie helpless in bed while the nurse read it to her. She knew from the first word what was coming. Ben Hale had ruined her. He had taken chances with her money and with other people's money, and he had lost. Ben Hale, she learned, had had to drown himself in the end. He hadn't intended to hurt anyone; Kate knew that. She had always liked him in spite of herself, even when he was not playing quite fair with her.

Tomorrow his bank would not open its doors. The padlock would stay all day on its iron gate, while within the bank examiners looked through the books and found out to a penny how much Kate and the others had lost.

Kate sent the nurse away because she wanted to think. She had to figure things out before Pauline came home. She didn't know what to say to her daughter because she was not sure how Pauline felt about young Harry Hale. For all Kate knew she might be in love with him. If so, that would make it very hard, for the extra had said that Harry Hale was determined to make good what his father had lost. Fool, thought Kate, fool—to undertake a task like that. It would mean a lifetime wasted.

For a long time Kate lay there and beat with her good hand on the blanket. She was a large woman—her toes touched the foot-board—and she had once been powerful. No one had been so strong as Kate. And now she was as helpless as a child. The thought made her furiously angry. This was a blow beneath the belt. It had caught her when she couldn't defend herself. A dirty trick. Low.

Kate heard a car come up on the driveway but she didn't at first pay any attention to it. Voices came through the open window.

"Well, Pauline?" That was Hoke Weatherby.

Pauline spoke hurriedly. "I can't give you any answer now, Hoke. Please don't ask me to. I'm going in to Mama." The engine started again and before it had died away Pauline was in the room. Kate lay perfectly still watching her. In the light of this new calamity Pauline's beauty was something that hurt. Pauline was tall, like Kate, but much slenderer. She hadn't had to work with her hands and her arms and her back, and she was graceful where Kate had been rawboned and awkward. Kate watched, fiercely, the gesture with which Pauline tossed her gold-colored evening cloak on a chair. Pure grace. Dancing, no doubt, had something to do with it.

Pauline was wild about dancing and she was, they said, as good as any professional.

Kate saw herself as a young girl. She too had loved to dance, although she had had no country club to dance in. A barn had served, or a schoolhouse, or even a patch of prairie in the moonlight. If they had had no fiddle, they had whistled. Many a time Kate had done a washing in the morning and an ironing in the afternoon, and had danced all night. She had cared as much about it as that!

Pauline tonight was wearing her pale green satin gown. She sauntered across her mother's room, past the great oak office desk, past the mantel with its china ornaments, past the chest of drawers until she reached the easy chair by the bedside. Kate heard her sigh as she dropped into it and picked up the extra which lay on the pillow.

Kate watched her in agony. Her money had bought that pale green satin gown; her money had kept Pauline's hair bright and soft and wavy, and kept Pauline's hands smooth and her cheeks pink and her body free. And now . . .

"Hard luck, Mama," said Pauline.

"All my life," cried Kate fiercely, "it's been like that. Hard luck and hard luck and hard luck."

Pauline leaned back lazily and moved a white finger across the pale green satin of her knee. Kate could hear the faint scratching of her nail. Pauline sighed.

"What I can't stand now," Kate went on, "is to be tied here like this. Not to be able to do anything about it. Always before I've been able to do something."

Pauline's brown eyes were hazy as though she wasn't half thinking about what had happened.

Kate began to recount the blows life had dealt her. "I was born to worse than nothing," she said, always fiercely. "We never had anything—not enough to eat or wear. Sometimes we didn't have any house; we went from place to place and lived in a wagon. I've been all over Texas in a wagon. Well, I worked out of that. I had to. I brought up the children after Ma died, and I helped Pa when there was anything to help him about and I did odd jobs for people, washings and such. And then, when the children were grown and I might have put myself through school, I married your papa."

Kate's eyes, which had been fixed on the china ornaments on the mantel, traveled back to her daughter.

"That's one way out," said Pauline without looking up. "Marrying."

"Out!" repeated Kate bitterly.

Then it occurred to her that Pauline had not been thinking of her father but of herself. "I've thought of that myself," said Pauline.

"What do you mean?" asked Kate. "Hoke Weatherby?"

"Why not? He's very rich."

"Yes, he's very rich."

"Something's got to be done."

Her words reminded Kate of the many times she had said them herself. "Something's got to be done." It was that necessity which had made her marry Pauline's father. She had been fond of him, of course, too fond of him perhaps; but it wasn't because of that she married him. It was because he was very ill and there was nobody else to take care of him. So Kate had gone on the eve of her marriage to the Quick Lunch Café to ask for work. She had been desperate.

"They gave you a job, of course."

"Yes, they gave me a job waiting on tables. I found a room over the drugstore where your papa could be quiet and sit in the sun while I worked."

Kate did not tell her daughter much about those days. She had a feeling often that Pauline would rather not know to what straits she had been driven to keep the two of them alive. And gradually Pauline's papa had grown fat, although as long as he lived he was never able to do much work. That didn't matter so much, as Kate saw it; the important thing was that she had accomplished what she had set out to accomplish.

"And then you had me," said Pauline.

Yes, she had had Pauline. That had been in a way another blow. And because of Pauline she had had to give up the restaurant.

"When I found out what was the matter with me," she said to Pauline, "I didn't know what to do. I walked up and down the streets almost all night. Your papa didn't know where I was and he started out to look for me. When he found me I was sitting on the grass in the little park we had then, planning a boardinghouse. I remember how we sat there side by side in the dark and talked about it. I had to do something. The next day I talked Ben Hale into letting me have what money I'd need, and before night I'd found a house that would do."

"I remember it," said Pauline.

Of course Pauline remembered it. She had lived there until she was five years old.

Kate had just paid off her mortgage and had begun to make a little money when the boardinghouse burned to the ground during a norther. There was no fire department in those days, and no hope from the first. It had all happened like a flash. Kate had been wakened by a little dog, and she had grabbed Pauline and shaken Pauline's papa, and shouted up the stairs to the guests, who were all asleep. For fear someone hadn't heard she had run up there herself, once Pauline was safe outside, and she had dragged an old man all the way down with the flames licking her heels.

"That was when we went to the Texas Hotel, wasn't it?" asked Pauline.

"I had to," said Kate. "There wasn't any other house in town big enough for boarders. I've always thought they cheated me in that deal, Pauline, but I couldn't see any other way out. I had both you and your papa to support, and then your Uncle Mo came to live with us. I thought he was going to be a help to me but he was old and couldn't do much."

"He and Papa used to sit on the porch, I remember," said Pauline.

"I made money on the Texas," said Kate. "I just made up my mind that I had to. I worked like a dog to do it but I didn't care. I never minded work."

"And then?" prompted Pauline, as if anxious to get the whole story straight.

"And then," said Kate, "Hoke Weatherby's brother shot your papa."

"Of course I remember that," said Pauline.

Kate could not escape her recollection of the scene. Her mind simply would not pass over it. They had been playing cards, and Pauline's papa had said that Hoke's brother was cheating. Kate had heard the scuffle from the kitchen where she was frying steak for dinner, and she had shut Pauline in the supply closet before running in. She had been just a minute too late.

Nor had his death been the worst of it. For she found out presently that he had borrowed money on the Texas Hotel, borrowed it to gamble with. Five thousand dollars. Kate had been fond of him and the truth was hard to bear.

"I didn't know what I was going to do," she told Pauline. "The Texas had only twenty rooms and I sat up all one night figuring how to keep going and pay off that debt. I didn't see any way at all to do it unless I had a bigger place. That's why I went to Ben Hale again and made him lend me the money to build a new hotel that would be big enough to pay."

"The Southern was a nice hotel," said Pauline.

"It was hard sledding for about five years," said Kate. "But after that I made money—all I needed. You know what I sold out for."

They were both quiet for a time after that because the sale of the Southern brought them down almost to the present. Kate had sold it only five months before, when her stroke make it impossible for her to manage it any longer. Not that Kate cared so much about herself . . .

"But I thought I was safe," cried Kate in a terrible voice. "I thought we would always have what we needed and that my being sick wouldn't make any difference. I wouldn't have believed this could happen. It's the thought that will kill me, Pauline—not being able to do anything about it."

"If I married Hoke," said Pauline, looking very intently at the ceiling, "we would have all we needed. He'd take care of you."

Kate twisted painfully in bed. "If I could only think!" she cried. "Then I could find a way out. But I can't put my mind on it, Pauline. I'm no good anymore. But I'd die before I'd let Hoke Weatherby take care of me. I couldn't bear that."

"At any rate," said Pauline, running her fingers through her hair, "we'll stick together, you and I."

Stick together? Kate had never dreamed of anything else. Of course they would stick together. And yet Hoke Weatherby . . . she had just said she would rather die . . . Kate knew now that she had to look ahead.

When she found her solution she was so weak that she could scarcely speak. She barely whispered, "I shall go to the poor farm, Pauline." Even then she knew that the solution was imperfect: it didn't provide for Pauline; it only relieved Pauline of the care of her.

Kate was surprised at the way Pauline took the proposition. Pauline got up from her chair and stood by the bedside, looking down on her mother. "Don't be a goose," she said. Her forehead, usually so smooth, was puckered between the eyebrows as if she were thinking hard. Kate knew the feeling. She knew too how it felt to clench her fist as Pauline clenched hers presently when she walked over to the mantel and beat for a minute or two on its polished surface.

Fascinated, Kate watched her daughter. She seemed in some

way to anticipate everything Pauline did. She knew well enough what Pauline was going to say over the telephone. It was almost as if Kate herself had willed it that way. "Hoke?" said Pauline very calmly. "I can't do what you wanted. No, I can't explain. I can't do it. Good-bye."

Pauline called another number. Of course. Kate had been sure that she would. "Harry?" Kate heard her say, "Harry? Can you come? Yes, dear, right away. There's something I want to say to you."

"Pauline," cried Kate, "what are you going to do?"

"Do?" repeated Pauline, coming over to her mother. "Why, I'm going to make Harry Hale marry me, Mama. After that it will be easy. I know it will. I'm not afraid. I'm going to open a dancing school right here at home. We'll get along some way. We'll have to. The nurse will have to go, of course, but I can take care of you myself. Maybe you don't know it, Mama, but there's money in dancing, if you go at it right. I have all sorts of plans in my head."

Bending down from above she looked to Kate taller than ever before, and stronger.

"Whatever happens, we'll stick together," said Pauline again, in a voice Kate had never heard before, although she knew precisely how it felt to speak like that.

It meant that Pauline wasn't afraid of anything. It meant pluck, determination, patience, faith. Kate knew all about it. She felt the hot tears in her eyes, in her ears, on her pillow. She was ashamed to be caught crying like that, but she couldn't help it.

"You see," said Pauline, "you don't have to worry anymore. From now on I'll do the worrying. And listen, Mama, I don't mind it a bit; I have an idea that it will be rather fun."

"We're fools both of us," said Kate. She knew that her voice was absurdly tender but for once she didn't mind.

Windfall

Although the well had come in soon after midnight, and it was now the middle of the afternoon, Cora had not seen it. At first she was afraid she would be in the way. Afterward, she was too busy in the kitchen, for besides her own family she had the crews to feed, and six or eight oilmen who couldn't take time to drive thirty miles to town for their meals. And immediately after dinner, the girls, who were sometimes willing to help her, went off to the well and left her alone with the work. "I'll go down when I finish the dishes," Cora promised herself.

By the time the work was done, however, she was tired, soiled, and sweaty, and the pasture was full of people who had driven in to see the well. She would have been ashamed to go down as she was. "I'll get cleaned up after a while, and then I'll go down," she thought, as she threw the scraps to the chickens gathered around the doorstep.

With the empty bucket in her hand she stopped for a moment in the doorway, under the newspaper fringe which rattled in the hot wind, and gazed into the far corner of the pasture. She could not see the well from the house; she could only see the mast of the drilling machine and the shiny new storage tank rising above the cluster of cars and people. Luke, she knew, was there, and her three girls, and her two boys, and most of her neighbors, for it was Sunday, and no one was working in the fields.

She went through the kitchen and into the bedroom. It was fully as hot as the kitchen, but it was dark, except for the pattern of

99

the sun on the cracked window shade, and there was a bed to lie upon. Cora sat down on the edge of it and took off her house slippers. Her bare toes felt as though they had been glued together with the heat. She stretched them, and rubbed them with a towel she found on the floor; then she lay down on the crumpled sheet with her hand on her cheek.

Now and then, while she rested, she rubbed the side of her nose, or the corner of her mouth, or her neck. She was very tired, and this was the first time she had had the bed to herself since the drillers had come, three weeks ago, and had taken the other bedroom and the other two beds. The girls had moved in with her, and the four of them had lain, night after night, across the bed in a row, with their feet hanging over the side, while Luke and the boys had slept on pallets spread down on the kitchen floor.

Cora got up after a few minutes and began to put the room in order. The girls had gone off without making the bed or picking up their clothes, and Cora had to hang their pink nightgowns behind the curtain in the corner, and stuff their stockings in the dresser drawers, and empty the slop jar, which had stood all day full of dirty water, and wipe out the bowl and the soap dish before she could bathe herself.

The cool water made her feel a little better. She sat as long as she dared with her feet in the bowl, but she knew she must hurry if she were to see the well before supper, so she dried herself, after a moment, and put on her clean underwear and sprinkled a very little of the girls' talcum powder on her neck and arms.

When she had put on her black shoes and stockings and her gray gingham dress, she took her sunbonnet from its nail in the kitchen and went outside. The chickens were still scratching about in the yard, and stepping into the muddy patches where she had emptied the slop jar. They came running up to her, but she shooed them away. She crossed the yard, passed the barn, skirted the wheat stubble, and entered the pasture.

II

Cars were standing everywhere, like shiny-backed beetles, in the sun. She could smell the hot leather, and the grease and the paint. When she came nearer, she saw the people—the city people, first, spreading rugs in the shade of their sedans, and drinking ice water from thermos jugs, and eating sandwiches and reading the Sunday papers. A little farther on she saw the country people—the men with their suspenders crossed on their backs, and the women with their flowered hats and their black shoes and stockings.

Cora did not really want to speak to any of them. She was always timid in a crowd, and conscious of her sunbonnet and her gingham dress, and lately, since she had lost her teeth, she was ashamed for anyone to see her mouth. They saw her, however, and would not let her pass.

"Say," they said, all of them looking her up and down, "you won't be speaking to us, Mrs. Ponder, now you've got a well on your place. You and Luke will be too good for us poor folks."

Cora stood shamefaced with her fingers over her mouth. "Oh, I don't know," she said. She was very much embarrassed. "I come down to see it myself."

But she could not see it just then, because the men were in the way. There were oilmen from town, with khaki breeches stuffed into their high boots, and East Indian helmets perched on their heads; there were farmers with creases in diamond-shaped patterns on their necks; and there were men in overalls, dodging the others while they worked with pieces of iron pipe.

"When they move to one side," she thought, "then I'll go over and see it."

Meanwhile she must find her girls. She didn't like to have them running around in a crowd like this with nobody to look after them. It wasn't right. They were dancing, when she found them, some time later, dancing on the grass with boys she didn't recognize. There was a phonograph playing and they were dancing . . . on Sunday afternoon! Cora was uneasy, and yet she didn't have the heart to stop them. They looked so pretty with their curly heads and their bright dresses and their silk stockings and their fancy kid slippers. She watched them for a time, standing beside an empty automobile, but if they saw her, they gave no sign of it.

She walked back to the country women at last, and sat down with them on the grass, pulling her skirt carefully over her knees. "I wouldn't mind seeing that oil with my own eyes," she said. Yet she did not like to intrude where the men were gathered. They were all laughing and talking and spitting on the ground, and she knew they would be uncomfortable if she joined them. They would clear their throats, and mumble good afternoon, and touch their hats. And Luke would frown at her.

She saw Luke now, hobbling around and smiling foolishly at his neighbors, as though this well were some joke he had played on them. And she saw Whitney, her younger boy, in his bare feet and dirty overalls, helping the men with the pipe. The older boy was nowhere to be seen. Cora sighed, because she was afraid he had gone off somewhere with one of the girls. She had seen him change his shirt, after dinner, and shave, and oil his pompadour, but she hadn't dared to ask him where he was going. He wouldn't have answered her, probably, if she had.

The women among whom she was sitting began to ask her questions. They wanted to know what she would do with the money from the well. Cora answered them with her hand over her mouth. "I don't know," she said, feeling her face grow red. "I don't rightly know what we'll do." She did not like to speak of her teeth, and yet she could think of nothing else she particularly wanted. "We might get a phonograph for the girls," she said at last.

The women were astonished. "Why, haven't you got a phonograph, Mrs. Ponder? You haven't! Nor a radio, neither! Well, what do you know!"

"We might get a radio, too," said Cora.

"Those girls of yours will sure spend the money, Mrs. Ponder. You can leave it to them."

Cora stiffened at that. "I'd be glad for them to spend it," she said. "I've never been one to begrudge things to my children."

They shook their heads at that, and said it wasn't always a good thing for children to have too much. "They don't have the respect for you they should have, Mrs. Ponder."

Cora looked at the ground. "I know," she said; "I know." She was beginning to wish she had not come down to the well. She might have known the women would be like this. And yet what they said was true enough. She had spoiled her children, and often she was sorry and ashamed. She ought to have made them help today with the work. She ought to have made them stop dancing . . . on Sunday, too, where everyone could see them. And it was true, what they said, that the girls would have had more respect for her, instead of always being ashamed of her. And yet . . .

"They'll want that you should move into the city; that's what they'll want," said one of the women.

Cora winced, because that very thought had been troubling her all day. "It's not likely that we'll be moving to the city," she said.

"They'll want a fine house in the city, Mrs. Ponder," said another woman, "and lots of parties and dancing."

Cora did not answer, and presently they left her alone.

She had nothing to do. She watched a red ant travel through the grass with a bit of wheat in his mouth. She watched a cricket scamper past on his high stilts. Finally, she pulled a blade of dusty grass and sucked it, and watched the cars stream into the pasture from the main road. There were Fords filled with farm boys, and smart roadsters from the city, and trucks with the dust as thick as moss on their greasy wheels. They left the gates open and drove where they liked, breaking down the limbs of the mesquite, and staining the grass with drippings of black grease. The crowd was everywhere, trampling the cotton in the next field, climbing through the barbed-wire fences, peering into the barn, chasing the chickens in the yard, and marching into the house, even, to use the telephone.

Cora saw the people from the next farm drive up in their tour-ing car, with the idiot boy gaping on the back seat. When they climbed out he followed them about like a foolish dog, grinning at everyone he met. From the back, in his new gray suit and his straw hat, he looked like anyone else; it was only when you saw his face, or his gait, that you suspected.

A few minutes later she saw Jasper Gooley drive up in his blue and yellow coupe. She had known Jasper when he was a boy on his father's farm, long before anyone knew there was oil under the cotton. Old Mr. Gooley had been the poorest of them all. All his life he had lived in a one-room shack, with no paint on its boards, and no grass in the yard, and no trees—not even a red cedar to break the wind in the winter or to give a little shade in the summer. It was just a bare shack standing on posts, so that the chickens could run underneath to get out of the sun.

Jasper was a boy then, like her Whitney. Cora used to see him lazily chopping cotton, in ragged overalls and a torn Mexican hat. Once she passed him, on her way home from town, lying on his back in the ditch, where it was shady, and he looked up at her and laughed. That was before he was old enough for girls.

Cora wondered sometimes what would have happened to Jasper if there had not been oil on his father's land. He would have had to stay at home, then, and run the farm, and make a living, and no doubt he would have settled down like his neighbors, with a wife and a family. Instead of that he had rented the farm to tenants. The very week after his father's death, Jasper had rented the farm and had gone to the city. People shook their heads now when they spoke of him. They said that he was wild, that he drank, and that he al-ways had one woman or another on the seat beside him when he drove on the country roads. They said he had had an affair with a married woman in town that had cost him ten thousand dollars in cash. Perhaps it was true, and perhaps it wasn't; Cora didn't know.

At any rate he had a woman with him now, a large blonde woman in a red hat. Cora saw her squint in a little mirror while she dabbed powder on her nose. She saw Jasper's Panama hat, and his fat hands resting on the wheel, and his puffy cheeks; and when he climbed out of his car, backward, she saw his blue-and-white-striped seersucker trousers, and his white silk shirt and his white shoes.

She was glad when Jasper passed her by without speaking, for she never knew how to act with city people, or what to say to them. It suited her much better to follow them at a little distance as they made their way toward the well. Now that Jasper had brought a woman among the men, she didn't mind going nearer.

III

She could see the pipe now, sticking up from the ground, and bending over at the top, and she thought she saw a black stream flowing into the tank below, but Jasper stepped in front of her before she could be sure. She stood behind him, one hand supporting her elbow and the other supporting her cheek under her sunbonnet, waiting for him to move.

She felt a little guilt. She knew that Luke would think she ought to go back where she belonged, yet she did want to see the oil. She wanted to see what it looked like. She felt as she did sometimes at funerals, when she wanted a last look at a face she had known, yet hated to push herself forward.

She was feeling more and more out of place when she saw Whitney coming toward her, stepping over pipes and wrenches, and elbowing the crowd. Even in his old clothes, she thought proudly, he was the best-looking of her children. The others were all a little too thin and sharp-featured, but Whitney was going to be broad and handsome, and sure of himself. He came up to her now, before everyone, not caring what they thought.

"Say, Mama," he said, "did you see the oil, did you?"

"No, son, I haven't seen it yet."

"Come on, then, and look at it."

He took her straight up to the tank. "Look in there, Mama," he said.

Cora glanced quickly about her to see if anyone disapproved before she dared to lean over the rim.

"See it?" asked Whitney.

She saw it . . . thick black oil, with a dirty scum on the top. The smell of it made her feel sick at her stomach.

"I see it, son; I see it."

Just then a sudden stream gushed from the mouth of the pipe, green in the sunlight. Whitney took her hand and held her finger in the stream.

"You taste it, Mama," he said eagerly.

Cora touched her finger to her tongue. It tasted like kerosene, and she had to spit it out on the grass.

"It's oil, Mama," said Whitney. "See?"

"Yes, son, it's oil."

He wanted to tell her all about it. "They think it's going to make a hundred barrels," he said. "And they're going to drill another one over yonder where you see the stake."

"Yes, son, yes."

"And after that they're going to drill to the south. They're going to drill a lot of them."

"I see."

Cora was beginning to feel very uncomfortable. She felt conspicuous, standing here where everyone could look at her, with no teeth in her mouth, and the oil still greasy on her finger. She had to stoop, at least, and wipe it off, secretly, on her stocking. Even then a little of it remained, black under her nail.

She was really glad, at last, to find an excuse to back away from the men. She saw part of a newspaper impaled on a mesquite thorn, beyond the well. She walked over to it, without attracting anyone's attention, and picked it up. Then she saw a scrap of shiny brown

106

paper and a wad of tinfoil, and beyond that, in a clump of cactus, a piece of sandwich wrapping, streaked with yellow salad dressing. There was an empty bottle lying under the wrapping, and bits of broken glass shining here and there all over the pasture. "Tomorrow," thought Cora, "after the washing is finished and on the line, I'll bring a bucket and gather it up before the cattle get into it."

On the top of a little rise, not far from the house, she stopped and looked back at the well. Luke and Whitney, she saw, were talking to Jasper Gooley. Jasper had his left hand on the shoulder of the woman he had brought with him from town; and as Cora watched, he crossed one white foot over the other and put his right hand on Whitney's shoulder. Whitney stood tall under his weight. Cora wondered, with fear in her heart, what Jasper was saying to her son.

Luck

Roy was sitting on a table in the back room of the domino parlor, waiting for something to turn up, when he heard about the accident on Mr. Cox's well. The derrick man had lost his balance in the wind and had fallen off the platform and landed on his head on the derrick floor. Mr. Cox had just brought him in to the hospital.

Roy slid off the table and buttoned his lumber jacket over his flannel shirt. Then he stuffed his hands into his pants pockets and hitched up the street toward the hospital. He didn't wish anybody any bad luck, but an accident was an accident, and a job was a job, and if there was work to be had, even on one of Mr. Cox's dry holes, he might as well have it as the next fellow.

Sure enough, when he had passed the undertaking parlors and cut through the filling station at the corner, he spotted Mr. Cox's muddy Ford, parked in front of the hospital between a Lincoln sedan and a new Packard coupe. There were plenty of old Fords in the North Texas oil fields, but Roy could have picked Mr. Cox's out of a whole lot of them. Her top was gone, and her fenders were cracked, and one of her springs was broken, so that she hung on a slant, and a stream of rusty water was dripping from her radiator. The old bus had sure seen service.

Mr. Cox hadn't come out yet.

Roy let himself down on the running board, which creaked and sagged under his weight, and dug his heels into the mud. He might as well take things easy while he waited. He yawned, and rubbed his eyes, and blinked at the sky. It didn't look so good. A stiff north wind had been blowing down from Oklahoma all afternoon, and it looked like rain. Lord! If there was one thing they didn't need just now, it was rain. It had been raining almost steady for three weeks and the roads had been growing worse every day. You could hardly get through in anything but a Ford. Most of the operators weren't even trying to get through. They had shut down their wells, instead, and turned their crews loose in town until things dried up.

Mr. Cox hadn't shut down, though, and Roy was willing to bet anybody ten to one that he wouldn't shut down, no matter how long it rained. No, sir! You couldn't scare that bird with a little mud. Not him! Especially if what Roy had heard was true, and Mr. Cox, for once in his life, was on an oil sand.

Roy tucked his fingers under his cuffs and leaned farther forward to get away from the wind, which was cutting the back of his neck. If it kept on like this, they were likely to get snow instead of rain.

He had laughed, yesterday, when he heard that Mr. Cox was on a sand.

"Not that bird!" he said to the barber who told him about it. "He don't hit no sands, Cox don't!"

But the barber stuck to his story. He had it straight from old man Rouse, who had brought in four big wells on the next lease. Rouse had seen the cuttings, and the scum of oil floating on the mud of the slushpit, and he had told the barber that Mr. Cox was setting casing in the hole.

Roy didn't know whether to believe it or not. He'd like to see Mr. Cox hit a sand all right, but when a bird has drilled eighty-eight dry holes, one after the other, without bringing in a single producing well, you don't look for him to get a break, somehow.

"I'll bet you five dollars," said Roy, "that he don't make no well out of it."

But the barber wouldn't take him up. There wasn't a man in town, for that matter, who would have bet a nickel on Mr. Cox. They all knew too much about his luck. Nothing ever happened right for Mr. Cox. If he didn't run into salt water, he dropped his tools in the hole, or he lost his casing seat, or had his derrick blown down in a windstorm. He couldn't drill six inches without getting into trouble of one sort or another.

Mr. Cox might not remember it, but Roy had worked for him once, a couple of years ago, on a well he was putting down in the middle of the Burton pool, and he knew something about the way things framed up on Mr. Cox. He was in trouble all the way down. First it was his rig. The machinery kept breaking down and he had to send to Oklahoma City for parts. Then he ran onto a boulder which rolled over everytime he managed to drill through it. Then he began dropping things in the hole. Five hundred feet of drill pipe twisted off, one night, when he was pulling the tools to change the bit, and the next day he lost a fishing tool and another string of drill pipe on top of that; and then, as if that wasn't grief enough for one well, he sent to Tulsa for a hydraulic jack, and lost one of the cylinders off it.

It was hard luck, all right, but Mr. Cox was used to that sort of thing, and the next week he spudded in another hole on the same lease. He had plenty of trouble on that one, too, but he got to the bottom after a while, and then, as luck would have it, he missed the sand. There he was, in the middle of one of the biggest pools in South Texas, without so much as a rainbow in the slushpit!

Roy had to hand it to Mr. Cox for one thing, though: he never hollered about his luck. He always wore a poker face, and you couldn't tell by looking at him whether he cared one way or the other. He was the same way when he gambled in the domino parlors or when he shot craps with the boys on the derrick floor. Roy had seen him cleaned out plenty of times, but he had never yet seen him bat an eye. He might grin a little and show his teeth, but that would be the end of it. He wouldn't crab or cry on anybody's shoulder, not Mr. Cox! They said in the oil fields that he had been a prizefighter before the war and that he could stand more punishment than any fighter in the Southwest, and Roy believed it. Punishment was his middle name. You'd think he liked it, the way he always came back for more.

Eighty-eight dry holes, and still going strong! You couldn't get a bird like that down. As soon as he finished one dry hole, he got busy on another. And he worked like a nigger. You'd see him standing in some farmyard with his feet apart and his hands in his pockets, arguing with a farmer about a lease he was trying to block up. You'd see him stuffing circulars through the letter slot in the post office. You'd see him sitting in a restaurant, with his maps spread out on the sugar bowls and sauce bottles, trying to make a deal with an oilman as broke as himself. You'd see him in the supply houses, trying to talk the managers into giving him credit. You'd see him standing on the hotel corner, buttonholing everybody who came past. You'd see him tearing along the roads in his Ford. And then, the first thing you knew, you'd see him rigging up in some pasture or cotton patch where nobody ever thought of drilling before. You'd see him driving stakes with a sledgehammer . . . breaking the ground for his slushpit with a pickax . . . hoisting derrick timbers, like one of his own roughnecks. He'd be everywhere at once for the next three or four weeks, until he abandoned that hole and started all over again on another. Some hustler!

Roy wished to God he'd get busy and do a little hustling now. What do you suppose was keeping him in the hospital? Trying to patch up his man himself, was he?

And good Lord! There came the rain! A cold drop hit Roy in the eye, and he wiped it out with his knuckle. Another one landed on the back of his hand . . . on the brim of his hat . . . on his shoulder. A minute more and it was spattering down as if it meant business. Zowie!

Roy stood up and picked his way through the mud to the sidewalk. Wasn't that Mr. Cox's luck, now? . . . another . . . and rain . . . and him in a car without any top to it!

Roy hunched his shoulders and climbed the hospital steps to a

112

little roofed-over porch which was built on the front of it, and sat down on the railing. Through the glass panel in the door he could see what was going on inside. A nurse was trotting up and down the hall and an old man was trying to get a drink from the water cooler. Mr. Cox wasn't anywhere around. Once Roy thought for a minute that he saw him coming, but it was a young fellow in overalls, instead, with one kid in his arms and three more of them hanging to his pants legs as if they were scared to death.

Roy yawned. He leaned back and against the corner post, where he could look through the windows and see the patients lying in bed, and crossed his feet on top of the railing. In one room a poor son of a gun had his leg trussed up in a harness that hung from the ceiling. In another, a man was sitting up with a white mask over his face, with slits for his eyes and nose and mouth. Roy had seen them like that before. That bird was burned; that's what was the matter with him. A boiler had burst, maybe, or a well had caught fire, and he had got burned. Maybe he'd get over it and maybe he wouldn't.

Wait a minute! There was somebody else coming down the hall, and this time, by God, it was Mr. Cox. No mistake about that. He was talking to a doctor in a white coat, and he stood for a minute just inside the door, scratching the back of his head, with his mud-spattered hat dangling from his hand. Then, all at once, he slapped his hat on his head, and thrust out his long, crooked jaw, which always made Roy think of a fishtail bit, and threw the door open and bolted down the steps.

"Hey! Mr. Cox!" Roy dropped his feet to the floor and caught up with him on the sidewalk.

"Looking for me, are you?" Mr. Cox looked bad. His eyes were bloodshot, and his face was yellow and pasty under his sprouting beard.

"I sure am."

"Well, what do you want? What in hell do you want?" Already the rain was running off his hat and his rusty leather coat.

"I heard you was a man short on your well," said Roy.

"Yeah." Mr. Cox let his jaw drop while he scratched the corner of his mouth.

"How about taking me on, then?"

Mr. Cox didn't answer him right away. He waited until a truck with a storage tank chained to its back had sloshed up the street; then he walked all the way round his Ford and kicked the tires to see if they were holding up; then he swung his boots over the door, and slid into his seat and turned the switch.

"Crank her for me, son, will you?"

Roy stepped into the mud and braced himself against the radiator while he heaved the crank over. The motor sputtered and choked. Suddenly it began to roar.

Roy jumped back out of the way.

"Pile in if you want to," said Mr. Cox.

II

As the car jumped forward, Roy climbed in beside Mr. Cox and sat down gingerly on the springs which stuck up through the upholstery. Then he turned up the collar on his lumber jacket and pulled his hat as far down as it would go on his head. They had a cold, wet ride ahead of them.

With the soft mud spattering in all directions, they ploughed up the street past the hotel, the supply houses, and the stores.

"The roads ain't so good," said Roy. "Have any trouble bringing your man in from the lease?"

"Yeah, I had a little trouble."

"Didn't go in the ditch, did you?"

"No, I didn't go in the ditch."

"Hurt pretty bad, was he?"

"Yeah."

"Think he'll get over it?"

"Not hardly."

"That's tough luck."

"Yeah."

At a gray stucco filling station with orange trimmings at the edge of town they filled up the leaky radiator and put four gallons of gas in the tank under the seat.

"That ought to take us out and back," said Mr. Cox, grinning a little and showing his teeth.

"Sure," said Roy.

He could see that Mr. Cox was broke . . . flat broke. That was why he got only four gallons of gas instead of filling his tank. As it was, he lacked two bits of having enough to pay for it.

"I'll tell you what I'll do, son," he said to the boy. "I'll come by tomorrow and give it to you, see?"

They went on down the road, with the rain blowing in their eyes and the mud splashing on the windshield. At the refinery they had to wait while a string of round-bellied tank cars was shunted back and forth on the railroad tracks. Then they plunged down a slippery hill and slued around the corner at the bottom.

"Damn that mud!" said Mr. Cox, through his teeth.

The boss was about done in. Roy could see that all right. Whenever he touched Mr. Cox's knee, he could feel it shaking. And the old boy blew up over nothing at all. Every time they slued on a curve, he seemed to think he was going in the ditch, and began making faces and jerking the wheel around. Once, when they were driving past an old slushpit where somebody had drilled a dry hole, a ball of tumbleweed blew down the road and stuck in the rut ahead of them, and Mr. Cox dodged it as if it had been a boulder, and came near throwing Roy over the car door.

"Say!" said Roy.

"What's the matter?"

"Nothing ain't the matter of *me*."

A few minutes later the car slued again and righted herself just in time.

"I bet you been sitting up nights with your well," said Roy.

"I'll say I been sitting up nights with my well."

"Haven't had any sleep, eh?"

"Not much."

Birds like Mr. Cox, who drilled on a shoestring, never had time to sleep. They were all the time trying to make deals. They had to, as far as that went. They had to trade interests in their wells for everything they needed . . . for hauling and fuel oil and board for their crews. And Roy had an idea trading wasn't so easy when nobody wanted their interests under any circumstances.

No sir! Roy didn't know where Mr. Cox had got hold of the casing he had set in his well, but it was a safe bet that he had done a good deal of sweating and swearing before he found anybody who would trade with him. And then, Lord! The mud! He must have had a sweet time hauling that casing to the lease. Load a truck and a trailer down and see how fast you can go through the mud!

Oilmen were all the same. If they weren't making deals, or traveling back and forth to town, they were standing around on the derrick floor, smoking cigarettes and getting in the way of the crews. Maybe, when nothing much was happening, they'd double up on the seats of their cars and go off to sleep for a while, but they'd be back before long. Roy had noticed that a man couldn't sleep very long at a time when he needed a well as bad as Mr. Cox needed this baby. He had too much on his mind. He'd be afraid all the time that his casing wouldn't be right, or that he'd drop a string of it in the hole, or that they'd get nothing but salt water for all their trouble when they bailed.

No sir, Mr. Cox hadn't eaten a square meal, probably, or slept in a bed, or taken his boots off since he ran onto that sand four days ago, and what's more, he wasn't likely to eat or sleep or take his boots off until he found out just what was at the bottom of his well. And maybe not then.

Roy yawned and leaned forward to let the rain that had collected in the brim of his hat run off onto the floor between his feet.

A little stream of water found its way inside his collar and ran down his chest under his shirt. Another twenty minutes and he'd be soaked to the skin, back and front, unless the wind turned cold enough to change the rain to sleet. Not that sleet would help matters much . . .

The radiator boiled and spit steam back on the windshield as they pushed along in low gear past the fences and the clumps of rotten cactus and the bare mesquite trees. Roy was sick of looking at mesquite. It was all the same size and shape, and it was all twisted the same way. Now and then he saw a steer that had drifted down to the fence and was standing there with its nose between the wires and its tail to the wind, or a farmhouse set up on blocks, with a muddy water tank in the yard and the dead cotton stalks standing in the field, or a weather-beaten derrick on a hill. Once they saw a yellow Buick lying wheels up in the ditch.

"Trouble for somebody," said Roy.

"Yeah."

Mr. Cox had gone only about half a mile further when he got into trouble himself. He met a fuel-oil truck crawling toward him in the ruts. The driver stopped in the middle of the road and waited for Mr. Cox to turn out.

"Damn that bird!" said Mr. Cox.

He swung the wheel to the right, but the old car was as contrary as a mule. She wouldn't leave the ruts. Then, suddenly, she skidded and slued and started to slide sideways.

"Hold her!" yelled Roy.

Mr. Cox stuck out his jaw, and jammed his foot down on the brake, and swung the wheels the other way, and she slued again, halfway around this time, and stopped short, crossways of the road. The engine choked and sputtered and died.

Roy jumped down in the mud and cranked her. Then he tugged at the spokes of the front wheels . . . kicked the tires . . . heaved on the fenders. Then he waded around to the back and pushed while the wheels spun around and churned the road in his face.

"God!"

Mr. Cox rocked her back and forth, and suddenly she started forward.

"Hold her . . . she's sliding!"

The old fool! Why didn't he head her back into the ruts? Why didn't he stop?

Roy scrambled for a footing on the bank. He tried to hold her up with his weight, but he couldn't do it. No sir, he couldn't do it. She was too heavy for him and the bank was too slippery. She hung for a minute on the edge, and then she began to topple. He'd better get out of the way, and he'd better do it in a hurry.

He jumped back into the ditch and pulled himself up the bank on the far side.

Mr. Cox was trying to get out from under the steering wheel. He couldn't make it. He didn't have time. There she came over! There went Mr. Cox, clear of the car, sprawling in the mud! There she lay, in the ditch, with her four muddy wheels in the air!

"How's that for luck!" said Roy.

III

It was snowing.

About dark, when a farmer with a team of mules was dragging them out of the ditch, the rain turned to sleet, and half an hour later, when they stopped to change a flat tire, the sleet turned to snow. The wind was still blowing a gale. One minute you'd see the road, and the next you wouldn't see anything except a flurry of snow which stung you in the eye and took your breath away.

Mr. Cox was having a sweet time keeping to the road. The wind was all the time beating him over to the left, and besides, he couldn't see where he was going because he had only one headlight. The other had been smashed when they turned over in the ditch. A little thing like that didn't make any difference to Mr. Cox, though. You'd think, to watch him, that all he cared about was getting out to his lease, and if he broke his neck getting there, why, that was all right with him.

Roy, however, had had enough of it right now. He didn't know why he had ever started out with Mr. Cox. He must have been crazy. A guy was crazy to start anywhere on a night like this, and he was worse than crazy to start anywhere with Mr. Cox.

Roy had been a damn sight better off before he had a job. At least he hadn't been sitting out in a blizzard in a car without any top, with a wet shirt freezing to his back and a pair of mud-soaked shoes freezing to his feet. He'd say he hadn't! And the prospects of a night's work ahead of him in the cold!

"How're you coming?" asked Mr. Cox.

"Not so good," said Roy.

"It won't be long now," said Mr. Cox. "That's Rouse City ahead . . . that light."

The fine snow blew down inside Roy's collar and melted on his neck as he leaned over the door. So this was Rouse City, was it? The last time he had been out here there wasn't anything at the crossroads but a soft-drink stand where they sold corn liquor on the Q.T. Now there were filling stations and houses and restaurants and machine shops and lumberyards, all because old man Rouse had brought in a new pool down the road a ways.

At the crossroads, where a couple of trucks were parked with their trailers folded up on their backs, Mr. Cox turned to the right, and this time he got around the curve without any trouble.

"Road's beginning to freeze, eh?" said Roy.

"Yeah."

"It's sure getting cold."

"Well, what of it? What do you want me to do about it?"

"Nothing."

Mr. Cox slowed down, suddenly, and began poking his head around as if he were trying to get his bearings in the snow. Then he swung the wheel sharply to the left, and thumped over some loose planks which made a bridge over the ditch, and stopped short, with the nose of the car against a barbed-wire gate.

"Get out, son, and open the gate," he said to Roy.

Roy swore as he stepped down on the planks and edged along the car to the fence. The wind flapped his stiff pants against his legs and swirled the snow in his face like sand in a sandstorm. He couldn't get his breath, and he couldn't see what he was doing, even when he had scratched the mud from the headlight. And the wire tore his hands as he fumbled for the gatepost. Lord! There, he scratched himself again on the back of the hand. He wiped the blood on the seat of his pants. Then he jerked the gatepost out of the loop, floundered around for a minute in the half-frozen mud, ducked under the limb of a mesquite tree which he hadn't seen before, and stood shivering in the rustling snow while Mr. Cox drove through the gateway.

Then he had to hook it up again, without so much as a headlight to help him this time, and he came near to slipping into the ditch. Everything felt like everything else to his numb fingers. He couldn't tell whether he had hold of the fencepost or the wire or his own arm. Finally he lit a match with his fingernail, and grabbed the loop as the flame flickered out, and jammed the gatepost into place.

"Come on," said Mr. Cox. "Hurry up and climb in."

"Lord!" said Roy. His pants had frozen stiff and they cracked like boards as he bent his knees. "Lord, I can't see in the dark, can I?"

Mr. Cox pulled down the gas throttle, and the car began to bounce and jolt in the deep, crooked ruts. Roy hung on to the door with both hands. They seemed to be in the middle of somebody's lease . . . old man Rouse's, likely, and there wasn't any road . . . nothing but these crazy zigzag tracks through the fields. They ran over cactus and yucca and pieces of iron and boards. Then they passed close to a powerhouse, with light showing around its door, and Roy thought he could make out a battery of storage tanks against the sky, and the walking beam of a pump jerking up and down.

"Whose well's that? Rouse's?"

"Yeah."

"Rouse is sitting pretty, eh?"

"Yeah."

Some birds got all the luck, and Rouse was one of them. It didn't make any difference where he happened to drill; he always got a well. He could put down a hole ten miles from the nearest production and get a thousand-barrel well. He could take a lease that was spotted all over with dry holes, and find a new sand nobody had ever heard of before.

Rouse drove a blue Pierce-Arrow, and lived in a two-story brick house with a red tile roof and scalloped shades at the windows, and you could see him any day, almost, lying back in a chair in the hotel barbershop while the barber patted his face through a wet towel, and the manicure girl filed his nails, and the nigger rubbed polish into his cordovan field boots. Afterwards, he would elbow his way through the lobby in his cowboy hat and his leather coat and buy himself a big cigar and light it with the gold outfit he carried in his pocket.

He had every damn thing he wanted, Rouse did. He had a box at the ball park, and a string of polo ponies, and a cellar full of whiskey and gin, and a hunting lease near San Antonio, and he wore a diamond as big as a strawberry on his little finger. They said in the oil fields that Rouse could buy out the whole town and never know the difference.

"He's drilling an offset over there to the north," said Mr. Cox.

Roy squinted into the wind and made out the thin, whitish lines of a steel derrick in the distance. Everything was dark, though, and there wasn't any steam up.

"Shut down, ain't he?"

"Yeah, he's shut down. It got too cold for him."

It was too cold for anybody, as far as that went.

They jolted down a hill, splashed through a mudhole at the bottom, and chugged up the side of another hill, with one cylinder missing. Then they scraped through some mesquite, jounced, suddenly, over a waterline running to some tank Roy couldn't locate in the dark, and started up still another little rise. From the top of it

Roy saw a lighted derrick standing up to its knees in steam, and a pair of fuel-oil torches flaring under their black boilers.

"That your well?"

"Yeah; that's my well."

As they drove up, they could see the crew huddled around a stove of some sort on the derrick floor. The driller . . . he was a tall bird with a big nose . . . came out to meet them, and leaned on his elbows on the door by Mr. Cox.

"What say we call it a day?" he began.

"What do you mean, call it a day?"

"How about shutting down? It's too cold to go on working."

"You boys ain't fixing to walk out on me, are you?"

"Well," said the driller, "we wouldn't be sorry if you was to quit. I'll say that much. You can't go on drilling in a norther like this, Mr. Cox; you sure can't. The water tank will be froze over by morning."

Mr. Cox kicked the door open so suddenly that he came near to knocking the driller flat on his back.

"Listen here," he shouted, as he climbed stiffly down to the ground. "I wouldn't quit if hell was to freeze over."

IV

Roy couldn't see that the crew had so much to complain about. They had nailed up a lot of boards of keep the wind out, and they had made a stove out of an empty gasoline drum, and had connected it with the fuel-oil line, and they had a quart or so of corn whiskey which didn't taste half bad to a man who had been facing a roaring blizzard all the way from town in an open car.

It was plenty cold enough, though. The derrick floor was covered with ice, and the wind blew in through the cracks, and piled the snow in drifts in the corners. Roy thawed and steamed for a good while, and then he dried himself out, a little at a time, holding one foot and then the other up to the stove, and turning around and around in the heat. Now he was stamping his feet and flapping his arms and biting down on his teeth to keep them from shaking.

So far there hadn't been any particular excitement. They had let down the bailer and pulled it up again, and Mr. Cox had bawled everybody out because there wasn't enough of a showing to make a well, and then he had told them to drill on down a little farther into the sand.

"Dry?" said the driller.

"Hell, yes," said Mr. Cox. "Dry."

Dry drilling was a good deal easier than filling a sixteen-hundred-foot hole with mud and bailing it out again a few hours later, but even so, the driller didn't much like the idea. He was a family man, with a reputation in the oil fields for never taking chances unless he had to, and he had seen a gusher come in once, near Beaumont, when they were drilling dry like this, and burn ten men until nobody could tell which was which.

"Think you're going to get another gusher, eh?" said one of the men.

"No; I don't think I'm going to get another gusher."

"What's eating you then?"

"Nothing."

"He wants to go home and get his asbestos suit," said Roy.

The driller told him to shut his mouth. Then he walked over to the stove, where Mr. Cox, with the mud plastered all over him, was shivering and rubbing his fingers, and said something about turning out the fire.

"You can leave that to me," said Mr. Cox, and he turned his back on the driller.

Mr. Cox didn't look so good. He looked as if about all he wanted to do was to lie down on the floor and sleep for a week. And he couldn't seem to get warm. All the time they had been lowering the tools in the hole, he had been standing by the stove, kneading his hands, and kicking his ankles, and spitting on the floor, and not paying much attention as usual to what was going on. They had been feeling along in the sand for half an hour now, and Mr. Cox had hardly moved.

"I wish to God it would quit snowing," he said suddenly to Roy.

"Why? A little snow don't hurt nothing."

"Yeah, but the roads!" said Mr. Cox. "You can't drive through no drifts, son."

"I ain't planning to drive through no drifts."

Mr. Cox spit on the floor. "Yeah," he said, "but suppose I want to get a storage tank out here in a hurry!"

"You ain't going to need no storage tanks," said Roy.

"I wouldn't be too sure, if I was you," said Mr. Cox, and then he marched over to the rotary table and told the driller to pull the tools.

"I got a hunch we gone far enough," he said.

"What you say goes," said the driller.

Mr. Cox couldn't wait. "Get up in the derrick, you," he said to Roy. "What's holding you?"

"I'm going," said Roy. "I'm going, ain't I?"

As he started up the ladder, he heard the driller hollering about the stove again.

"Didn't I say I'd look after the stove?" Mr. Cox was shouting. "Didn't I say I'd turn it off in plenty of time? Didn't I?"

"I guess you did, all right."

"Then for God's sake shut up about it."

Roy fought his way up the ladder. Everything was coated with ice . . . the rungs of the ladder and the derrick timbers, and the planks of the platform on which he had to stand, with nothing but a strip of corrugated iron to protect him from the wind. It wouldn't take much to carry him off; that was a fact. The wind would swoop up from below, and then, before he had caught his breath, it would come back at him from the open side of the derrick. The strip of iron would bang, and the timbers would creak. And with all that snow in the air, he couldn't see half the time what he was doing.

Sometimes, for a second or two, there wouldn't be any snow,

and he would see the roughnecks heaving on the chain tongs, and the driller with his hand on the brake lever, and Mr. Cox leaning over the stove. The next second he wouldn't see them at all, but he would see the pink mud in the slushpit behind the derrick, and the two black boilers with the steam pouring out their stacks. Then another gust would swirl the snow back in his face, and he would have to feel for the drill pipe as it rose from the hole, and fumble for the side gate which fastened the elevator, and trust to luck as he swung the stand of pipe in its place in the corner of the derrick. If he lost his balance . . . if he made a wrong step . . . well, he was gone, that's all.

It was bad business all right, and it was slow. One sixty-foot thribble, and then another sixty-foot thribble, and then another sixty-foot thribble . . . and sixteen hundred feet to go! Roy's fingers were so stiff he could hardly bend them, and his eyeballs felt as if they were freezing over. Well, he didn't have anybody but himself to thank. He'd walked into it himself. He ought to have known better. He ought to have known that if he took up with Mr. Cox he'd get into something like this . . . or worse.

The snow was blowing the other way now, and he leaned over to see what was going on below. The driller had left his post by the rotary table and he was walking kind of stiff-legged over to the stove. Roy was too high up in the derrick to be sure what was wrong, but he could see that Mr. Cox was leaning back in the corner of the derrick. The son of a gun looked as if he had gone off to sleep on his feet. Anyhow, the driller stooped over as if he were turning off the fuel oil, and he began to shake Mr. Cox by the shoulders.

After that, Roy didn't pay much attention to Mr. Cox, or the stove either, for that matter. He was watching the next thribble come up from the hole. He saw the driller throw the brake, and he saw the roughnecks toss the slips which held the pipe from dropping around it and start to break the joint.

Half a second later, he saw something else. He saw a thin stream of oil spurt sideways from the joint. Boy! There had been oil standing in the hole! And it had worked its way up inside the hollow drill pipe! Mr. Cox was likely to make a well out of it yet!

Yeah . . . but the stove! the stove! Roy caught his breath. God! If the oil sprayed on the red-hot stove!

"Hey!"

There was a roar, and a sheet of flame and a cloud of black smoke and another sheet of flame, which flashed in his face and sizzled his eyelashes.

"Christ!"

Somebody screamed, and he saw the driller running through the fire with his arms out in front of him.

The slushpit! Where was the slushpit? He'd have to jump for it! He ducked under a cross brace, swung out from the derrick . . . peered through the smoke until he caught sight of the slushpit far below . . . and jumped.

His neck snapped as he struck bottom. Then he fell on his face, and fought for his breath as the mud filled his eyes and nose and throat.

V

Roy felt somebody pull him out and drag him along the ground. He lay there awhile, sneezing and choking and spitting mud, as sick as a dog.

Somebody trampled on his hand.

"Where's Cox?"

There was so much mud in his ears that everything sounded a long way off.

"He's over here. Roll him over again."

"Get a doctor. Get an ambulance!"

"Ambulance! You're crazy! How can I get an ambulance?"

"Where's the Ford? Somebody start the Ford."

"You damn fool! Can't you see the Ford's on fire?"

"Don't touch him anymore."

"Leave him alone."

"Look at his face!"

"Yeah; I see it."

Roy wiped the mud out of his eyes. He could begin to see a little. He got up on his knees and blinked at the blazing derrick. Something was moving in front of him, and he saw that it was a man dripping with mud and holding one hand over his cheek. There was another man sitting in the grass. He didn't have any hair or eyelashes or eyebrows or any skin on his face, and he was staring at his hands as if he didn't know what it all meant.

Roy knew what it meant! It meant that he didn't have a chance in the world.

The man looked up suddenly, and grinned, and showed his teeth.

"Son," he said, "I'm going to make a well out of it . . ." And Jesus Christ! It was Mr. Cox!

Roy crawled over to him on his stomach. Yeah, it was Mr. Cox, all right; it was Mr. Cox, burned so bad he couldn't feel anything. When you were burned like that you were done for. You wouldn't know it, but you were done for just the same.

Roy's throat was full of mud again, and he leaned over to spit into a bunch of yucca. Then he began to bawl. He bawled like a baby, and he couldn't stop.

"It's your luck," he heard himself scream at Mr. Cox. "It's your goddamn luck!"

Mr. Carmichael's Room

Mrs. Philips couldn't put Mr. Carmichael out of her mind. Not that he was any kin to her . . . not that he had been easy to get along with, either, in the ten years he had been living at her house; but somehow, when you have had to put up with a man for that long, and have tended him when he has been sick, and picked up after him every day, why you can't help feeling it when he dies. And to walk in on him like that, not even knowing he was sick, and find him dead in the bed with his clothes on and his eyes open—well, as she had said to the undertaker a little while ago, it was too bad, that was all; it was just too bad!

There was a good bit of work to be done this morning around the house, but it seemed like she couldn't get to it. The water pipes, which had been frozen up tight for the last five days, had thawed out in the night, when the wind dropped, and she could have started in on the dishes stacked on the drainboard, or she could have taken the broom and swept out some of the sand which had sifted in on top of everything, but here she was instead, shivering in her winter coat, and rocking herself back and forth in the porch swing like it was the middle of summer, while she waited for long distance to locate Mr. Carmichael's daughter in Dallas.

She could have stayed inside, of course, where it was warmer, but she didn't like to, somehow—not this morning. And now that the norther had blown itself out, it sure felt good to have the sun shining on her back again. It was the first pretty day they had had for going on two weeks. Well, if it kept on like this, the grass, what there was left of it after the hard freeze, would turn green, and the burning bush and sunflowers and one thing and another would come up in the vacant lots, and it would be time to plant turnip greens.

Just now, though, the neighborhood looked pretty well frozen up. Most of the front-room shades in the bungalows across the street were still down to the bottom of the windows—folks stayed in their kitchens or their bedrooms mostly in cold weather—and the hydrants in the front yards were still tied up with gunnysacks or pieces of quilts or what not to keep them from freezing and bursting, but there were a few people, like herself, who weren't afraid to stick their noses out of doors and breathe the air. She saw a plumber crawl out from under a house with a blowtorch in his hand and go off in his truck, and she saw a lady in a man's overcoat and a lace boudoir cap trying to get her car started in the driveway, and having a time with it.

Well, anyone was likely to have trouble with a car after a norther. Take the old Chevrolet, now, that Mr. Carmichael used to drive around winter before last. It was always freezing up, and the only way he could get it started was to pour boiling water through the radiator and lay hot cloths on the carburetor. Many and many a time she had heard him swearing at it, with his stiff red hair standing on end and his hands so cold he could hardly manage the teakettle.

Mr. Carmichael hadn't had to worry much about a car this last year, though—not since the company he bought the Chevrolet from had taken it back. Mr. Carmichael had been good and sore about that, but it was like she said to him: he wasn't doing any drilling, and what did he want to bother with a car for, anyhow? No, it was just the notion of not having a car that hurt Mr. Carmichael. He had got used to a car when the oil boom was on, and he didn't know how to manage without one; that was all.

The undertaker had asked about it the first thing. Did Mr. Carmichael have a car? Did he have a drilling rig? Did he have any leases he hadn't drilled up? Did he have a typewriter? Or a gold watch, even? Mrs. Philips didn't much like him. Undertakers had to look out for themselves, she supposed, but with Mr. Carmichael . . . well, it didn't set right, somehow.

You could say what you had a mind to about Mr. Carmichael, but he wouldn't have tried to get a dead man's car away from him. He sure wouldn't. Mr. Philips remembered when her brother was killed . . . ran into a piece of pipe sticking out behind a truck parked in the road, and died before they could get him to a hospital. Mr. Carmichael, now, didn't even know her brother, but he had tiptoed into the parlor, just the same, where she was rocking with her handkerchief up to her nose, and he had sat down on the edge of a chair, and turned his hat around in his hands like he was looking for a hole in it, or a stain, or something.

"We don't none of us know when it will be our turn next," he had said, in his big, hoarse voice which he never could tone down, somehow. She always told him he talked like he was yelling to a roughneck on the other side of the derrick. "Now, if there's anything I can do, Mrs. Philips—if you need any money, or anything at all, why you just let me know, see? No ma'am, we don't none of us know when it will be our turn next."

Well, it was Mr. Carmichael's turn now, and all the undertaker was interested in was how much he was going to get out of it. And even Della Mae, likely, wouldn't waste any grief on her daddy. Her mama would see to that. For since Mrs. Carmichael had got her divorce and married the automobile salesman in Dallas, she was dead against Della Mae having anything to do with her daddy.

Well, it was just too bad, that was all; it was just too bad.

Mrs. Philips was sorry, now, that she had asked him to go after that bucket of water last night. And yet how was she to know he was feeling bad? He hadn't said anything about it, and he hadn't looked any different from always when he ducked under the kitchen doorway and eased over to the stove where she was heating up a brick of chili for her supper. He had had a glass in his hand with what looked like corn liquor in the bottom, and he had said he wanted some water to fill it up.

"You *would* ask for water, Mr. Carmichael," she had said, "just when the pipes are froze and the bucket's empty," and then, noticing that he still had his sweater on under his coat, and his boots, she had put it up to him. "How about fetching me some water from the hotel, Mr. Carmichael?" she had said.

Mr. Carmichael had stared down at her for a minute, and then he had swallowed his liquor straight, like it was, and without saying anything, he had grabbed up the bucket and clumped out through the back door. She remembered now that he had been all out of breath when he came back, and that he had taken another drink, without any water in it this time, either, but he had said, "Here's to Luck!" the way he always did, and ducked under the doorway again, and gone off to his room, just as usual. She had heard him coughing in the night, when the water started running and she had to get up to turn it off, but he had coughed in the night a plenty of times before and she hadn't thought anything of it. And then, in the morning, to walk in and find him dead!

And yet what could a man expect who wouldn't take care of himself? Mrs. Philips had warned him a plenty of times. "You're burning the candle at both ends, as they say, Mr. Carmichael," she had told him, and he had just laughed at her for her trouble.

Well, he wasn't so different from the rest of the oilmen she had seen come and go. Take during the boom, now, when he was making money faster than he could spend it: he never took a minute's rest. He'd sit up with a well all night, maybe, and then he'd no sooner get back to town than he'd start off for somewhere else . . . Tulsa, or Fort Worth, or San Angelo, and he'd no sooner get back from there, plastered with mud, likely, from his hat to his boots, than he'd have to tear out to the lease again to see what had happened while he was gone. He hardly ever used to sleep at home in those days, and there were weeks at a time when Mrs. Philips never once had to make up his bed.

Then, when things quieted down, and he ought to have begun to take life easy, it seemed like he went crazy trying to spend the money he had made. He joined the country club, and went to running around with a bunch of men who drank and played cards all the time. Mrs. Philips didn't know any too much about them, but she had an idea that Mr. Carmichael's new friends took a good bit of his money away from him, in one way or another. And if he wasn't playing cards, he was going to prizefights or wrestling matches, and laying bets on the winner, and getting into some little private fights of his own, too, because he used to turn up, sometimes about daylight, with his shirt torn half off him and his face cut up. Lots of days Mrs. Philips had found him asleep in bed, in the middle of the morning, with all his clothes on. "Why don't you kick me out of here, Mrs. Philips?" he would say, sitting up, and trying to find the floor with his feet. "That's what my wife did . . . kicked me out. Why don't you hand me my gun and tell me to bump myself off?"

No, Mr. Carmichael hadn't slept regular, and he hadn't eaten regular—not since he quit the hotel. While he was boarding there, he got a plenty all right, but he had a row with the manager about his bill and they wouldn't charge his meals anymore. Or that is what people said, anyhow. After that, he just ate when he happened to think of it. Days when he was promoting a well, and sending out circulars to his stockholders, he would sit all morning humped over his desk, without ever going out, smoking cigarettes and sprinkling the ashes on the floor, and punching the keys of his typewriter, one at a time, and scratching out his mistakes with his knife blade. Then, at dinnertime, maybe, he would go over to the Piggly Wiggly on the corner and come back with a paper sack, and, afterwards, she would find grease spots and crumbs of cheese and potato chips and sausage on the floor.

She didn't like it any too well . . . his eating in his room . . . but she never liked to say anything, for some reason, to Mr. Carmichael.

II

Mrs. Philips had left the swing and was standing by the porch rail, pulling pieces of dead morning glory vine out of the wire netting nailed to the posts, when she saw the hearse, with the undertaker on the seat, come up the road and stop in front of her house.

"Well, you're back again, Mr. Haley."

"Yes, ma'am." Mr. Haley stood on the steps and took off his felt hat, which was as big as a cowboy's and a pale gray color, almost white. Mr. Haley was a little man, side of Mr. Carmichael, anyhow, and his lip was hidden under a black mustache.

"Has the young lady called yet?" he asked pleasantly, and he pulled a big white handkerchief out of his hip pocket, under his coattails, and blew his nose.

"No, sir; she hasn't called yet."

Mr. Haley scratched the corner of his mustache. "How about this girl, now, Mrs. Philips? On the level, I want to know. Will she be coming on up, or won't she?"

"I couldn't say as to that."

Mr. Haley tapped his fingers on the porch post. "I've been making some inquiries around town," he said presently, "and I've been to all the banks. They've got plenty of notes on Carmichael, but no cash."

"Well?"

Mr. Haley hung his hat over his hip and scratched his head. He had slick black hair, cut short over his ears.

"What I'm getting at is this, Mrs. Philips; I want to look through his things," he said.

"Just as you say, Mr. Haley."

Mrs. Philips marched ahead of him into the house and opened the door of Mr. Carmichael's room. The shades were down, and the room was dark and cold and quiet as a grave. You could see the tracks, in the sand, where people had walked around on the bare floor, and you could see fingerprints on the chair by Mr. Carmichael's bed—as if he'd fumbled in the dark for the glass which was lying there, on its side, by the empty flask. He must have gone straight to bed when he left the kitchen, for nothing else had been touched. The sand was still thick on the dresser and the rolltop desk and the swivel chair, and the windowsills.

"If I'd a known when you was coming back, Mr. Haley, I'd a had the room warm for you," said Mrs. Philips, as she took a match from the wide mouth of a china bird on the dresser and knelt down in the dust to light the gas heater, which stood well away from the wall at the end of a red rubber hose.

Mr. Haley was making himself at home. He laid his hat on the counterpane, which had been pulled up over the pillow when they carried Mr. Carmichael out, and he stood with his feet apart while he lighted a cigarette.

"You see it's like this, lady," he said, squinting through the smoke and walking over, in the middle of what he was saying, to spit in the brass cuspidor Mr. Carmichael used to have in his office downtown. "I didn't go into this business for my health, see? I got to get something out of this, even if it isn't so much."

"I reckon you got to live like the rest of us," said Mrs. Philips.

"Yes, ma'am, I got to live; you sure said it."

"Mr. Carmichael, he was three weeks behind in his rent when he died," said Mrs. Philips, presently.

"That so?"

"Yes, sir; he was three weeks behind in his rent."

"It looks like he owed 'most everybody around town," said Mr. Haley.

"Yes, sir."

After a minute Mr. Haley went over to Mr. Carmichael's closet and opened the door.

"You won't find nothing in there," said Mrs. Philips.

He wouldn't, either, for a fact . . . just a lot of empty flasks and bottles she hadn't got around to carrying out, and some books Mr. Carmichael had bought from an agent during the boom, and what few clothes he wasn't wearing when he died—a pair of lightweight gray pants, and a ragged silk bathrobe, and his golf knickers and his hat, and his field boots. That was about all.

Maybe Mrs. Philips didn't hate to see Mr. Haley messing around in there! She couldn't help thinking how mad it would have made Mr. Carmichael, and how Mr. Carmichael would have knocked him down and trampled on him, if he had walked in on him.

Mr. Haley was examining the knickers. The moths had eaten some holes in them, but otherwise they were extra nice knickers. Mr. Carmichael had had them made to order in Dallas when the country club was first started, and he used to put them on on Sunday mornings and go off for the day with some of the friends who hung around him so much for a while, there. Mrs. Philips didn't know whether he really played golf or whether he just sat around the clubhouse playing pitch or poker or whatever it was that they played, but she knew he had sure missed the club since they had run him out. It seemed like he didn't have anyplace to go after that.

Mr. Haley kicked the books which were stacked up on the closet floor. "What did he want with all those books, do you suppose?"

Mrs. Philips couldn't say as to that. She had never seen Mr. Carmichael reading a book in his life and she didn't know why he had bought them unless some agent had talked him into it. There was one set, fancy books with leather bindings, called *Complete History of the World*, and another called *Secret Memoirs of the French Court*, and another called *Famous Speeches of History*, and they had all been piled up there in the closet for going on nine years now, with the dust settling on them and the mice gnawing the corners.

"I can't see where this gets us anywhere," said Mr. Haley, slamming the door shut.

"I told you there wasn't nothing in there," said Mrs. Philips.

III

Mr. Haley whistled as he strolled over to the dresser and studied himself in the mirror. His necktie was a little to one side, so he straightened it and stretched his neck out and drew it in again like an old hen. He was taking his time, and Mrs. Philips knew that he was hoping she would get tired of waiting, and go out.

Well, she wasn't going to do anything of the sort; she was going to stay right with him and see it through.

There wasn't anything on top of the dresser excepting Mr. Carmichael's old military brushes, with the bristles full of red hair, and his comb, and his razor, and shaving brush, and a silver cup his dog had won, once, at the dog show in Dallas. Mr. Carmichael was sure crazy about that bird dog . . . used to buy a big hunk of meat for him every night at the market and stand out there in the back yard, no matter how cold or wet it might be, watching him gnaw on it. And when the dog got distemper, Mr. Carmichael brought him in the house, and gave him a coat to lie on in front of the heater until he died. Then he borrowed a shovel and dug the grave himself, out by the alley.

Mr. Haley didn't notice the cup, though; he was going through the drawers. In one of the little top drawers there were some loose playing cards and some dice, and some red, white, and blue poker chips in a broken box, which seemed to strike Mr. Haley as funny.

"That's where they cleaned up on the old boy," he said, with a chuckle. "There's one bird down at the hotel who claims he won thirty thousand from Carmichael in one night, and I guess he did all right."

"Is that so?" said Mrs. Philips.

Mr. Haley took more time over the other little drawer, which was jammed full of all sorts of things. What Mr. Carmichael wanted all that stuff for, Mrs. Philips didn't know. He never used any of it, but that's the way he was: when he had money in his pocket, he spent it, and he'd buy anything he saw, or anything the next fellow bought, whether he wanted it or not. Here, now, was a nice amber cigarette holder, and a silver shoehorn, and a red-and-green silk scarf, with a knotted fringe, and a silver cocktail set in a leather case lined with velvet, and a bottle of French perfume, and another bottle shaped like a Chinese idol with pink bath salts in it, and his revolver, in a leather holster.

When he saw all that stuff, Mr. Haley perked up a bit. He slipped the cigarette holder into his pocket, along with the revolver, and he tossed the cocktail set on the bed with his hat. Then he clapped his hands together to shake off the dust, and started in on the two lower drawers.

The upper one had clothes in it . . . such as they were . . . some of them clean, and some of them dirty. Mr. Carmichael had been up against it lately: none of the laundries would take his washing. They'd send their drivers around to the house all right, with bills to collect, but when he tried to get them to take his washing they would just shake their heads and laugh and go off. Only last week, Mrs. Philips had caught Mr. Carmichael hanging up a dripping union suit to dry, over the back of his chair. He must have rinsed it out in the bathroom bowl, though it wasn't any too clean at that.

"I'll hang that out on the line for you, Mr. Carmichael," she had told him. He hadn't answered her, nor looked her square in the face, for the matter of that—just kind of growled as she walked out with it.

Most of the things in the drawer were dirty, but over at one side there were a few clean clothes—a couple of worn-out shirts, with his initials embroidered on the sleeves, a pair of hose with the laundry tag clipped to the top, and some pink silk pajamas, which looked like they had never been worn. But then Mr. Carmichael never wore pajamas anyhow; he slept in his underwear like anybody else. There was one handkerchief, too, which had been rinsed out and dried and folded up like a clean one, although there were brown stains all over it. Mr. Carmichael was always hard on his handkerchiefs. Even when he carried nice linen ones, he would use them to wipe the grease off his hands, or clean his windshield, or polish his shoes . . . anything like that . . . and they were always stained and dirty-looking.

The bottom drawer was all but empty. There were a few shotgun shells rolling around loose, and a fishline wound on a card, and an old plug of chewing tobacco which had crumbled all over the bottom of the drawer. Mr. Carmichael had been a great hand to go hunting, when he had money. He would go all the way to South Texas or New Mexico, and he would even cross the line into Old Mexico if he thought he could shoot a deer or a bear; and he had all the fixings—shotguns and rifles and cartridge belts and wading boots—everything you ever heard of. What had become of all that stuff, Mrs. Philips didn't know; he had either sold it, or gambled it away, or just given it to somebody, maybe. He was always lending things to his friends, and so far as she knew, he had never asked for anything back.

Mr. Haley tossed the stub of his cigarette into the cuspidor, and lighted another.

"You don't see anything here the little girl is likely to want, do you?" he asked.

"No, sir," said Mrs. Philips, "I can't say as I do."

IV

There wasn't anything left now but the desk. The other furniture in the room belonged to Mrs. Philips, but the desk was Mr. Carmichael's, and he used to have it in his big office in the Sinclair

Building. He had hauled it out to the house when he had to give up his office. What on earth she'd do with it now that he was dead, she didn't know—sell it, likely, for what she could get out of it, unless maybe the next roomer wanted it.

Mr. Haley shoved the rolltop up as far as it would go.

"If there's anything at all worth bothering about," he said, "it's got to be here."

The desk looked bare without Mr. Carmichael's typewriter, which the company had taken back a month or so ago. It wasn't much of a typewriter, maybe, but it was all Mr. Carmichael had to write his letters on, and he was good and mad when they carried it off.

"What's the use, Mrs. Philips?" he had said, running his fingers through his hair, as he sat on the edge of the bed. "I ask you now, what's the use?"

There was only a glass inkwell and a pencil tray on the top of the desk, and a picture of Della Mae in a silver frame. Although Mrs. Philips had seen it a plenty of times before, she picked up the picture and looked at it while Mr. Haley poked in the little drawers and pigeonholes. Della Mae was a right pretty little thing, according to her picture, with her hair all set tight and even in a marcel, and her eyebrows thinned out to nothing at all. Her lips looked a little too thick and black, but that was the lipstick, likely. Actresses' mouths in the movie magazines looked the same way.

The picture had been taken the first year Della Mae was in Dallas, and her daddy was sure tickled with it. "This here's my little girl; I got her in school in Dallas," he used to say to people who came in, and then, more often than not, he'd pour out a couple of drinks and shout, "Here's to Luck!" as he lifted his glass.

But then, Mr. Carmichael had always been wild about Della Mae. He had bought her a little Cadillac car of her own, and he used to go down to see her every chance he got, and take her places. Once, when she was sick with the flu, he had lost out on a deal because he wanted to see for himself how she was getting along.

Then every year he took her to the Dallas Fair, and the football game and the show, and he used to let her buy all the clothes she wanted and charge them to him. Then, come Christmas, he'd have Mrs. Philips go to town and buy a lot more stuff for her—silk underwear and hose and perfumes and such, and one year . . . it was just before he was kicked out of the country club, too . . . he had sent her a wristwatch with diamonds all around the face.

Lately, since times had been so bad, and the big companies had quit buying what little production he had left, and especially since he had lost his car, Mr. Carmichael hadn't done so much for Della Mae. It must have been two or three years, now, since he had gone down to see her, and in a way, you couldn't blame him much. He wouldn't have wanted to show up there, broke, without a decent suit to his back or a car or any money to spend on her.

Mrs. Philips lifted the glass and the flask from the chair by Mr. Carmichael's bed, blew the sand off the top, and dragged it across the floor to the desk, where Mr. Haley was leaning forward in the big swivel chair, sorting over what he had found in the little drawers and pigeonholes. It was rubbish, mostly, as she could have told him it would be—a few old sheets of paper with Mr. Carmichael's letterhead on it, half a dozen two-cent stamps, a dried-up eraser, a kodak picture of Della Mae in riding breeches, standing by a horse, and some Christmas cards tied up in bunches, each year by itself—1925, 1926, like that—cards folks had sent Mr. Carmichael in the mail. "Cheerio! The Season's Greetings! Mr. and Mrs. George Harper Groves" . . . "The Southwestern Supply Company wishes you a Merrie Christmas and a Prosperous New Yeare" . . . "The Ridgeview Country Club sends New Year's Greetings and invites you to attend the dance to be given at the Clubhouse on New Year's Eve."

Last Christmas there had been hardly any cards at all—just two or three from out of town. And there had been nothing, she remembered, from Della Mae, although Mr. Carmichael might not have noticed that, he was drinking so much.

And now Mr. Haley was beginning on the big drawers down below. She could see by the way he pawed through them that he was used to this sort of thing, and knew when a paper was valuable and when it wasn't. He didn't bother with the maps, nor the blueprints, nor the photographs of drilling machines and derricks, nor the oil well logs which always reminded Mrs. Philips of the color charts they showed you at a paint company. The letters seemed more in his line, although he tossed most of them on the floor as soon as he had glanced at them.

Mrs. Philips picked up a handful while she waited. Some of them were duns, but most of them were letters from Mr. Carmichael's stockholders, written on lined paper, in pencil. "We are sending you ten dollars, which is all we can raise just now. I have no work this week, but as soon as I get another job, will send you some more." . . . "I have heard about your company, and as I have a thousand dollars insurance money from my husband who was killed last January, I want you to take care of it for me. I have six children and I need some money bad." . . . "I want to know how soon you expect to begin paying dividends. Remember I borrowed on my house to send you the money and you promised to double it in thirty days and maybe less. I tell you it will mean trouble if I don't get something pretty soon." . . .

Mr. Carmichael had always been kind of ashamed of his mail-order business. Mrs. Philips remembered once when she had brought him in a lot of letters the postman had left. Mr. Carmichael was chewing tobacco while he colored little patches on a map with different colored pencils, and he had poked the letters around for a minute without opening a one of them. "If anybody drives up and asks you, Mrs. Philips," he had said, spitting out a mouthful of tobacco juice, "you tell them this is a hell of a way to make a living."

There wasn't anything crooked about Mr. Carmichael, though; she wouldn't believe that, no matter what anybody said, but it just seemed, sometimes, like he didn't know how to take care of himself.

He was always getting mixed up in things without half knowing what they were about—like the time he bought the stock in the bank, just before it failed. No, there might be mail-order operators who never expected to make any money for their stockholders, but Mr. Carmichael wasn't one of them.

Well, for once, Mr. Haley must have found something. He was sitting back in the swivel chair, grinning at a lot of papers clipped together at the top. It was Mr. Carmichael's sucker list. Mrs. Philips had seen it plenty of times, lying out on his desk . . . "J. K. Good, 2634½ Railroad Street, Topeka, Kansas . . . A. C. Daggett, General Delivery, Pittsburgh, Pa." . . . like that . . .

"Where did he get this list?"

"I couldn't tell you, Mr. Haley."

"He got a lot of answers, did he, when he sent out circulars?"

"Yes, sir, he always had mail coming in."

"The little girl wouldn't have any use for it, would she?"

"Not hardly," said Mrs. Philips.

Mr. Haley pushed back his chair and smiled at her as he slipped the list into the inside pocket of his coat.

V

They were looking through some letters from Della Mae, asking for this and that and the other thing, when the telephone rang. Coming as it did when everything was quiet except for the rustling of the papers and the grating of Mr. Haley's shoes on the sandy floor, it made Mrs. Philips jump like she'd been shot.

"That's her, likely," she said.

To save her life, she couldn't keep her voice steady as she answered.

"Hello."

"Are you ready on your call to Dallas?"

"Yes, ma'am."

"Here's your party; go ahead."

"Hello, is this Della Mae?"

"Yes, ma'am."

"Well, this is Mrs. Philips—where your daddy lives."

"Yes, ma'am?" Her voice sounded mighty little and far away.

"Well, hon, he died in the night."

"I'm sure sorry," said Della Mae, after a pause.

"Yes, hon, I was sure sorry myself."

"What was the matter with him?"

"Well, I don't rightly know, Della Mae. The doctor says his heart, most likely. He was just a-laying there dead this morning when I went in to make his bed."

Mrs. Philips could see Mr. Haley, in the doorway, trying to tell her what to say.

"What do you want we should do about burying him, hon?"

Della Mae was talking to someone. Mrs. Philips could hear them whispering.

"Mama says you'll just have to go ahead and bury him the best way you can," she said presently. "Mama doesn't want I should go up there, and anyhow I can't right now. We're going to drive to Houston tomorrow . . ."

"I see," said Mrs. Philips, "and you wouldn't feel like you could help me out a little? Your daddy was three weeks behind in his rent when he died."

Della Mae was consulting her mother again. "No, ma'am, I couldn't do that; I'm sure sorry."

"Or you couldn't help pay the undertaker?" added Mrs. Philips as Mr. Haley came closer.

"No, ma'am, I couldn't."

"Well, how about his things, hon? You wouldn't want I should send you any of his things?"

"Why . . . ," Della Mae was hesitating. "Well," she began again, suddenly, "did he have any money in the bank?"

"No, hon; he didn't; he sure didn't."

"Well," said Della Mae, "I don't guess you need to send me anything, then."

"Just as you say."

"I . . . I'm sure sorry," said Della Mae.

"Well . . ."

Mrs. Philips walked slowly back to Mr. Carmichael's room. "Well, that's that," she said, stooping over to turn the heater down. "I knew we couldn't get nowhere with Della Mae—not with her mama working on her."

"She didn't mention the list, did she?" asked Mr. Haley.

"No, sir; she didn't say nothing about the list."

"It wouldn't be any use to her anyway," said Mr. Haley.

After a minute, he took his hat from the bed, and juggled the cocktail set up and down before he stuffed it into his overcoat pocket.

"There are quite a few things you can turn in for yourself, Mrs. Philips," he said, looking around the room. "You can get three or four dollars for a pair of boots like that; and there's the desk, and the silk pajamas . . . and the silver frame on the little girl's picture . . ."

"Well . . . ," said Mrs. Philips.

"I'm going to run along now," he said, presently.

"Yes, sir."

"And I'll take care of the body all right; you don't need to worry about that."

"Yes, sir."

Mr. Haley hitched his overcoat up on his shoulders and tugged at the back of his velvet collar and slapped his hat on his head.

"Well, good day," he said at the door.

145

"Good day," said Mrs. Philips, following him out on the porch.

"It's sure a pretty day for a change," said Mr. Haley.

"It sure is," said Mrs. Philips, and because she couldn't stand going back into the house just then, she sat down in the porch swing, with her coat wrapped more tightly than ever around her, and watched Mr. Haley drive away in the hearse.

Fever in the South

M r. Donovan took one hand from the steering wheel and drew his watch from his pocket. It was twenty minutes after five. In an hour, or an hour and a quarter at the most, he ought to be in the capital of the East Texas oil fields. He let the watch slip back into his pocket, and took the wheel again in both hands.

He had been driving, in the rain, since the middle of the morning. Well, he was used to driving, had put more than sixty thousand miles on his car in two years; and he was used to mud, knew how to push through it. He hadn't spent twelve years in the oil fields for nothing. Still, he wouldn't be exactly sorry when he got into town. His arms ached from the strain of holding the car in the ruts, and he was sick of hearing the rubber finger of his windshield wiper squeak back and forth on the wet glass. It wasn't much good, really, in a drizzle; it only spread the mud, which splashed up whenever he met a car, a little more evenly over the surface, but it was better than nothing. Luckily there were few cars going west; nineteen out of every twenty were headed east, with Mr. Donovan.

Through the blurred wash of mud on the windshield he made out a red flag, presently, swinging from the end of a trailer. Another load of drill pipe bound for the oil fields—six-inch drill pipe, he saw, as he cut in ahead of the truck. Well, he had heard they were using six-inch in East Texas.

Ahead of him, as far off as he could see, were other trucks with their trailers, and other cars slithering along in the soft red mud.

Drilling rigs, which had been lying idle for a couple of years, likely in West Texas and Oklahoma and New Mexico, were moving in. He saw slush pumps and boilers and drill pipe and casing. And everything else that went with a boom—oil field workers in old Fords; promoters, like himself, in Buicks or Cadillacs; hamburger stands on wheels; wagons loaded with household goods; and all the way along, rain or no rain, the hitchhikers, with their coat collars turned up, and their paper bundles under their arms, begging for rides.

Mr. Donovan had seen the same thing plenty of times before—in Burkburnett and Mexia and Borger and Eldorado and Wink and Hobbs—but for once he couldn't warm up to it. He didn't trust it. He had been burned too many times in the last few years; and now that the big companies were down on him, and the government—now that you couldn't sell your oil even if you had it; well, he was through; that was all; he was ready to quit.

One thing he was sure of: he might look things over in East Texas; he might even block up some acreage and do a little trading; but he wasn't going to drill. He was through. He was broke, to begin with—flat broke—and he had more oil now than he could sell. No, the other fellows could gamble if they wanted to; he would keep out of it.

He ploughed on through the mud, slowing down when he had to, cutting in ahead when he could, never dropping under fifty miles an hour when he had a clear stretch of road. It began, presently, to grow dark. Through the slanting rain, he could see the pines ahead, on both sides of the road—East Texas pines. This morning it had been mesquite; this afternoon it had been oak; now it was the piney woods.

He began to see signs of the town. Here was pavement—an airport—a tourist camp—filling stations and grocery stores; then houses, after a while, and schools and churches and office buildings and hotels, and a courthouse, at last, in the middle of its square.

The streets were black with cars. Mr. Donovan saw licenses

from everywhere—Arkansas, Michigan, California, New York, Pennsylvania. It took him a good twenty minutes to find a place to park. And there were so many people on the sidewalk that he could hardly push his way through—not town people, either, but oilmen, geologists and lease hounds and mail-order promoters and drillers and, now and then, a roughneck, though most of them stayed nearer the fields. They looked mighty good, somehow, to Mr. Donovan. They looked like old times, before the oil business went on the rocks.

A hand came down on his shoulder.

"Donovan, how're you making it?"

"Not so bad!"

Yes, sir, it was like old times. Everybody was good-natured; everybody was hopeful; everybody was going to make a lot of money. There was a different atmosphere, somehow. It made you feel that maybe times weren't so bad after all.

Mr. Donovan squeezed along through the crowd. There was a beggar without any legs propped up against the wall of a building, holding out his hat. Mr. Donovan tossed him a quarter. Say, now, this was great! Here were fellows he had known years ago, in other booms, and forgotten. It sure seemed good to see them again. And they were all talking money. East Texas was the biggest field yet; you got oil wherever you went after it; you couldn't miss it; a man was a fool not to get into the play . . .

At the hotel, the lobby was packed to the doors and the crowd had overflowed onto the sidewalk. Mr. Donovan didn't even try to get inside. He knew what it was like, anyhow: under the haze of cigarette smoke the oilmen would be milling about, holding the maps up against the walls, scribbling down descriptions in little memorandum books, puzzling over abstracts. There would be map dealers, and brokers with blackboards, and a few women—geologists' wives, likely, swinging their boots from the rail of the mezzanine floor.

It was an old story to Mr. Donovan, and yet—well, it was beginning to get him. He couldn't help himself, somehow. It braced him up like a good stiff drink.

"Hello there, Donovan."

"Hello, Mac, how do things look?"

"They look mighty good, Donovan, mighty good."

"Suppose I can find a place to sleep tonight?"

"Try the Chamber of Commerce; they'll find you a room."

Mr. Donovan shouldered his way toward the café on the corner. Half of the crowd, it looked like, was broke and begging, and he was continually handing out nickels and dimes and quarters. "Here you are, son . . . No, I don't know where you can get work—just came down myself half an hour ago."

In front of the café, where the mob was huddled in the rain, Mr. Donovan fell in line. Through the window he could see the crowded tables, and the waitresses slapping down platters and swinging cups and saucers, and whenever the door opened, he could smell the grease and the onions and the coffee.

All around him they were talking about wells—twenty-thousand-barrel wells, thirty-thousand-barrel wells, fifty-thousand-barrel wells. Mr. Donovan found himself nervously scratching his hands. If a man only knew where to go now! If he could only count on his luck! If he could only get hold of a first-class fortune-teller— a girl like that Rita, up at Borger, who had told him three or four different times where to drill, and had hit it right, too, by God.

Mr. Donovan craned his neck. He had caught sight of a driller who had worked for him once in the Electra field. He whistled and shouted and presently he had him by the arm.

"Joe, how does it look to you?"

Joe was cockeyed with excitement. "Prettiest thing I ever saw, Mr. Donovan."

"Think it's going to hold up?"

"Sure I think it's going to hold up."

"You'd get into the play, then, would you?"

"Say," said Joe, "I heard you was quitting . . ."

"Quitting?" said Mr. Donovan. "Me quitting? Hell, no, I ain't quitting—not yet awhile."

II

It must have stopped raining sometime in the night, for the sun was shining when Rita woke up and looked out of the tent. Tom was up, ahead of her, and he was busy unloading the truck, and piling their things in the wet grass. Rita saw the red and yellow curtain she always hung over the tent door when she was telling fortunes, and her little table and her two straight chairs. Tom was sure a hustler. First thing she knew, he'd have the side of the truck propped up, and his tumblers and paper napkins out on the counter, and he'd be serving meals to the roughnecks.

Yes, it had stopped raining all right, but it was still wet here in the woods. Drops kept splashing down from the pine trees, the tent smelled musty, and the quilts were soaking, where they had dragged on the ground. Rita would sure be glad when Tom had time to set up the bedstead. All they had done last night, when they got to the oil fields, was to put up the tent, and throw out the bedsprings and the mattress and a couple of quilts.

They hadn't even taken off their clothes, they were that tired—only just their shoes and stockings. Well, that was all to the good; they didn't have to waste any time this morning getting dressed. Rita sat up and squeezed her bare toes into her sticky shoes. It wasn't any use putting on her hose; they were still wringing wet from last night. After a while, maybe, she'd have a chance to rinse them out and hang them somewhere to dry.

She ran the comb through her hair and felt her earrings to make sure they were safe. Then she ducked out from under the tent, and stood up and twisted her dress around where it belonged. After a while, when they got settled, she would tie her scarf over her head, so folks would know who she was.

"What's the matter with this place?" said Tom.

"There ain't nothing the matter with it."

It did look, sure enough, like they had picked them out a good place. They were so close to the wells that they could hear the steam puffing and they were right on the road, and they were in among a lot of other campers, who had to eat, she reckoned, like anybody else.

There must have been a thousand people, anyhow, camping along the edge of the woods. Most of them had tents, but some slept in their cars, it looked like, or maybe out on the ground; and they cooked over open fires. Every place she looked, Rita saw them squatting by their fires, trying to get the wet twigs to burn. On one side of her was a tent piled full of willow pieces—fern baskets and porch rockers and such. Well, Rita had never seen a boom yet where there weren't people selling willow pieces—and paper roses. On the other side was a sign painter. Rita could see his cans of paint and his brushes. She'd trade him a meal ticket, maybe, if he'd do her a new sign—"Madame Rita, Spiritualist"—to nail on a tree.

"Say," said Tom, "how about getting some water while I finish unloading, eh?"

"Where'll I get it? Out'n the creek?"

"Naw," said Tom, "I been there, but it's too damn muddy from the rains. There's wells around somewhere, though . . ."

"All right," said Rita. "Gimme the buckets and I'll get you some water."

With a bucket in each hand, she set out, presently, along the edge of the road. Except for the pine trees, which gave her a kind of shut-in feeling, this was just like all the other oil fields she had seen. There were the same horses, sweating and straining at their loads; the same oilmen honking behind them, trying to get past; the same wagons, with bedsprings and washtubs and oil stoves and crates of chickens; the same hamburger stands; and, as you came closer to the railroad tracks, the same signs—"Townsite lots, $50—Gas and electricity—high and dry"; and the same new pine shacks, with children standing in the doorways and women hanging the bedding out to air. There was the usual old fellow with a stock of rusty gas heaters to sell, and another with a load of furniture he had trucked in from somewhere—cots mostly, with a few chairs and tables.

Rita was mighty glad to see so much going on. She sure was. She liked a boom, anyhow. She liked the excitement. She liked the crowds, and the phonographs, and the smell of the coffee, and the rangers sitting on their horses with their guns in their holsters. And she liked the oilmen sneaking into her tent to have their fortunes told. She liked to see them sitting there, in the half-dark, listening to her talk. "You stand to make a lot of money if you work it right, but you got to watch out for somebody that's trying to double-cross you . . . There's something telling me you should go to the south. No, I can't see just where, only it's south and not north." It was a racket, that's what Tom said, but she had made some lucky guesses, and her clients had a way of always coming back.

Well, here she was at the crossroads. There were a few build-ings which must have been here before the boom, a drugstore and a café and a general store and a church—but all around, everywhere, were new pine shacks and corrugated iron warehouses. And cars! The cars were packed in so solid you could have stepped from one to the other clear down to the tracks without ever setting your foot on the ground. And sitting on the running boards and bumpers were the bums, all kinds of them, old fellows with whiskers and no teeth, the boys with thin white hands, and now and then an honest-to-God oil field worker out of a job.

Rita pushed through to a filling station. Sometimes, if an oil field town was big enough, it had a water system, and you could find hoses with faucets in the filling stations, but here there wasn't anything but a barrel, and the boy sent her off.

It wasn't any use trying the cafés or the hotels; she knew that. No, what she wanted was a farmhouse, with its own well, and she saw one, pretty soon, off to one side of town, in a grove of pines. At least it had been a farmhouse once; you couldn't tell what it was now, because there were rusty boilers lying out in the yard, and tanks and one thing and another, and a sign nailed to a tree saying "Bed and Board," and around by the well, there was another sign saying "Home Laundry," and a woman, running overalls through the wringer of a washing machine.

"Would you mind if I was to help myself to some water?" asked Rita.

"No, I don't mind. Go ahead if you want to."

"Much obliged," said Rita.

She walked back to camp the way she had come, slipping in the mud, now and then, and wasting water on the ground, but that was something she couldn't help. Anyhow there was enough left for the coffee, and she'd go back, after a while, and get some more.

"Say," said Tom. He had his little white cap on his head, and his apron tied around his waist, and he had come down the road to meet her. "You remember a bird named Donovan?"

"Sure I remember Donovan."

Tom jerked his thumb towards a muddy coupe parked on ahead, "That's him a-setting up there, waiting."

"Sure enough!"

"He seen me unloading," said Tom, handing her a red silk scarf and taking the buckets himself. "He wants you should tell him where to drill."

Rita wound the scarf around her head and tied it at the back of her neck. "Didn't I tell you they always came back?" she said; and she left the road and circled through the woods so that Mr. Donovan mightn't see her until she was ready for him. As for telling him where to drill, well, that ought to be easy, with all the oil there seemed to be in East Texas . . .

III

Moses had been messing around since sunup, patching his fence, and making him a gate out of the foot to an old iron bedstead a white man had traded him, a while back, for a load of firewood.

He was kneeling on the ground, studying how to fasten it to the gatepost, when he heard what sounded like a car a good piece up the road.

Moses cocked his head and listened. It was a car all right, and it was coming his way, through the piney woods. The hound dog growled and the children quit playing. They had been rolling tin cans down the slope in front of the cabin, but now they slunk up to Moses and stood gaping, with their eyes bulging out.

"What you scairt of, anyhow?" said Moses.

Fact was, though, he was scairt himself. Nobody hardly ever came to his place unless it was the laws, looking for stills, and Moses was scairt of the laws. He didn't have a still, but he was scairt of the laws anyhow. And he could see now that it was a sure enough white man in the car, and that he was turning in . . .

"You shet your mouth," said Moses to the hound dog. The children had run in the house to Lovie, and he could see them in the window.

He watched the car slow down for a mudhole and teeter up the slope and rock along towards him like it was fixing to run him down. Then it stopped, and the white man got out, and banged the door shut, and came walking over to Moses. He wasn't a law, though. He wasn't anybody Moses had seen up till now—a middling-sized gentleman, heavyset, with a wide felt hat and a leather coat and breeches and boots.

"Mornin', boss," said Moses, pulling his hat off and rolling it in his fingers.

"Your name Tatum?" asked the stranger. He had a short way of talking and Moses couldn't hardly follow what he said.

"Yes, sir, boss," said Moses, after a minute. "That's what I is called, sir—Moses Tatum, boss, that's what I is called."

The white man grunted. "My name's Donovan," he said.

"Yes, sir, Mr. Donovan."

Moses felt mighty low. He turned his hat around and around in his fingers. Out of the corner of his eye, he could see Lovie com-

ing out of the house—easing down the steps—limping along—
stooping over to pick up the hoe . . .

Mr. Donovan looked around him, all around him, this way
and that.

"You own this place, Moses?"

Moses took his time answering. He didn't know what to say.
Fact was, he was scairt to say anything. It seemed like white folks
made you say whatever they wanted you should say. He shifted his
feet and swallowed, and then he looked all around, just like Mr.
Donovan. He studied his house, with its mud chimney, and its gallery, sagging down where the blocks had rotted, at Lovie's black
boiling kettle, at her collard greens, at the old wagon, at the hogs, at
the chickens, at the mule, backing up to Lovie like he was fixing to
kick out at her, at his cotton patch, at his cornfield . . .

"Well, do you own this place or don't you?"

Lovie heard what Mr. Donovan was saying, and she stuck out
her underlip and wrinkled up her forehead. "Mornin'," she said.
Lovie was scairt of white folks, more scairt than any of them, and
she made her voice gross so as they mightn't know it.

"Yes, sir," said Moses, without looking at Lovie. "Yes, sir, I
owns my place."

"Where'd you get it? Buy it?"

"No, sir, I done inherit this land from my mama."

"How much do you own? Twenty acres?"

"Yes, sir. I owns twenty acres, that's what I owns."

"Your mother's dead, is she?"

"My mama's in the ground fourteen year come August."

"Any brothers or sisters?"

"Yes, sir, I done had seven sisters and six brothers."

"What's become of them?"

"They're in the ground, boss, ever one."

"All dead, eh?"

"Yes, sir, boss."

Lovie stepped up closer and leaned on the hoe. "What you fixin' to do, Moses?" she said.

Mr. Donovan laughed. "I'm fixing to make a rich nigger out of Moses."

"How you do that?"

"It's like this," said Mr. Donovan; "I'm fixing to drill a well, see?"

"We done got us a well," said Lovie.

"Not the kind I'm fixing to drill. I'm fixing to drill an oil well. I'll make a rich nigger out of Moses yet."

"No you ain't," said Lovie, and the hound dog at her heels began to grumble in his throat.

Moses coughed. "You shet your mouth. I wants to hear 'bout this oil well. What you mean a oil well, boss?"

Mr. Donovan sure talked fast. Moses had to pucker up his forehead and hold his head to one side and watch Mr. Donovan's lips mighty close to hear what he said.

"You don't make more than a bare living out here, do you, Moses?"

"I dunno, boss, I gets by . . ."

"Listen here, Moses, if you do what I say, you'll have more money than you'll know what to do with. I'm fixing to drill a wildcat, see? And I got to have around six hundred acres. It's up to you niggers to get together and meet me halfway. I'll play fair with you; I'll make you the best proposition I can, and then, if you're satisfied, I'll move my rig in and drill . . ."

"You wants to buy my place, boss?"

"No, I don't want to buy it; I want an oil and gas lease, that's all."

"I ain't looking for to sell it, boss."

"All you have to do is say I can drill, see? And then if I bring in a well, why then an eighth of all the oil belongs to you—provided your title's good, that is."

"What you say belongs to me?"

"An eighth. That's your royalty, see?"

"That's my royalty . . ."

"Sure. You'll be a rich nigger."

"And you ain't fixin' to put me off my place."

"No, I ain't fixing to put you off your place."

Moses twisted inside his shirt. He didn't see how he was going to make a trade with Mr. Donovan when he didn't understand what it was all about . . . a oil and gas lease . . . a wildcat . . . a eighth of the oil . . .

He looked helplessly at Lovie. She was turning the hoe handle round and round in her fingers, like she was fixing to run Mr. Donovan off the place.

"I dunno, boss," said Moses. "I got to study on it a while."

"What I better do," said Mr. Donovan, "is call a meeting of all you landowners in the schoolhouse. That's what I'll have to do. I'll call a meeting. I'll come back later and tell you when, see? I'll get you niggers all together and make you a proposition."

"Yes, sir."

Mr. Donovan climbed in his car and started his engine up so quick that Lovie like to have fell over the hoe.

"If anybody else comes along," said Mr. Donovan, leaning through the window, "you tell him you're tied up with me, see?"

"Yes, sir, boss."

Moses watched Mr. Donovan's car weave up the road between the pines. "What he mean?" he mumbled. "A oil well . . ."

Lovie's face was screwed up, and she was clutching the conjure bag she wore around her neck. "I dunno," she said. "I dunno. But he don't mean no good; that's sure. He don't mean no good."

IV

Although it was only the middle of the morning, Miss Carrie was so tired that her hands trembled and the blood thumped in her temples as she smoothed the counterpane over her bed. She had had very little sleep the night before. The telephone had rung every few minutes until midnight. "No," she had said, firmly, over and over again, "Mr. Donovan is not in, and I do not know when he will be in." Then, at a quarter after one, the geologist had awakened her, thumping up the stairs, and she had just been dropping off to sleep again when she heard Mr. Donovan. And at seven, the carpenters had begun to hammer and saw on the new apartment house on the corner.

Miss Carrie combed the hair from her silver-backed brush, rolled it around her finger, and dropped it into the hair receiver on her dresser. She knew that she ought to hurry. She knew that Mr. Donovan was waiting for her downstairs, and that he was impatient to get out to his well, but he would have to give her a little time. She was too old a woman to learn new ways, and she had to do things properly, oil well or no oil well.

Besides, this trip to the well was Mr. Donovan's idea and not hers—even though she was curious to see this oil which had already made such a difference in her daily life. Who would have supposed, two months ago, that she would rent out her guest room, with its old walnut furniture, or the other room, which had been her son's before he married? Or that Savannah would leave her, after sixteen years, to work in the hotel? Or that the town, where she had lived all her life in peace and quiet, would be so crowded with strangers that she would have to force her way through its streets? Or that the corridor of the red brick courthouse would be blocked with tables and chairs and girls copying records on typewriters? Or that the church where she had worshipped for fifty years would be sold to make room for an office building?

It was all very unpleasant, and Miss Carrie pressed her lips together as she lifted her hat from its box on the closet shelf and slipped her coat from its hanger. Of course she was glad, in a way, that prosperity had come to East Texas, but she could not help resenting the oilmen, who had swarmed in like locusts and settled on the town. There had been a steady procession of them for weeks now, knocking at her door, demanding room and board. Yesterday, one had asked if her parlor was full—and her dining room—or if she would be willing to screen off part of her front gallery with awnings and set up a cot for him there. And there were others— panhandlers, her son called them, who knocked at the back door, late at night, often, when she was alone in the house, and begged for food.

All of Miss Carrie's friends and neighbors had the same experience, and they all felt as she did about their roomers. Oilmen were so irregular in their habits; they kept such impossible hours; they neglected to lock the bathroom doors; they wiped their muddy boots on the linen towels; they brought strangers home to share their beds. You could never tell whom you were likely to meet, in pajamas, in your own hall. And of course there was the telephone, and the long-distance calls on the bill at the end of the month . . .

Miss Carrie drew on her gloves as she stepped softly down the stairs. She had been right about Mr. Donovan; he was impatient to be off, sitting nervously on the edge of his chair, twirling his hat in his hands.

He began to apologize for his car as he helped her down the steps. He had been carrying supplies to his well, it seemed, and the cushions were stained with mud and grease, but he would spread a newspaper for her to sit on, if she liked.

Miss Carrie braced her feet on the floor and held onto the door as Mr. Donovan swept around the corner and dodged through the traffic which filled the streets. How fast he drove! And how impatiently he honked when he had to wait at a crossing! Miss Carrie wondered what her son would say if he could see her now, sliding around on a newspaper, in a muddy car, with an oilman from West Texas . . .

She didn't see her son, however, or anyone else she had ever seen before. She saw oilmen, of course, hundreds of them, in their breeches and boots, and slovenly women carrying paper flowers from door to door, and boys selling sandwiches and pralines on the courthouse steps, and blind beggars, and old Negroes with guitars, but they were strangers, all of them, who had drifted in with the boom.

Even the buildings had changed. Almost every house had a new roof or a new wing. The church house stood empty, with its door swinging in the wind, and the parsonage was an office building. There were muddy cars parked under the blossoming peach trees in its yard.

Even the country, she noticed presently, as they crossed the railroad tracks and left the town behind them—even the country had changed. There were still green pines and pink redbuds and white flowering dogwood, in the distance, but all along the road, on both sides, were shacks and tents and corrugated iron buildings, and hamburger stands, and filling stations. And such people! Miss Carrie had been familiar with poverty all her life, but this wasn't poverty; it was something she didn't have a name for—something a great deal lower than poverty.

There were trucks on the road, loaded with what she supposed must be drilling equipment, and Mr. Donovan was continually blowing his horn and trying to pass them. Once he very nearly slid into the ditch, and Miss Carrie was thrown against the door as the car swerved around. A little farther on, a load of pipe had tipped over and they had to wait until it was righted.

Now that they were farther from town, the campers were fewer, and the shacks disappeared altogether. There was nothing for miles but the piney woods and the Negroes' little farms in the clearings, and their schoolhouses and churches and burying grounds. Ever since Miss Carrie could remember, it had been like this—a poor country perhaps, but dear to her, nevertheless.

"Now if you'll look over there," said Mr. Donovan, when they had been riding for an hour or so, "between those two tall pines . . ." He leaned over the steering wheel to point ahead. "You can see my derrick."

Miss Carrie looked. Yes, she could see the top of a great wooden skeleton, like an armless windmill tower, more than anything else.

161

The next minute, however, she lost it, for Mr. Donovan left the highway and turned off on a rough trail of some sort which wound down a hillside and across the bed of a creek.

"Just a few minutes now," said Mr. Donovan, "and we'll be there."

"There are no other wells in this neighborhood?" asked Miss Carrie. He had told her all about it, more than once, but she could never quite follow him, he talked so fast and about so many technical matters.

"No, ma'am, it's pure wildcat—no production within eighteen miles. It's funny about that," he added. "A fortune-teller, she told me where I'd hit it. That's the fourth or fifth time she's guessed right for me. It don't seem reasonable, but it sure works out . . .

"I got this particular lease from a nigger," he went on after a minute. "Told him I'd make a rich nigger out of him, and I would have, too, if he'd hung on, but he let some birds from Fort Worth talk him out of his royalty, a couple of days before the well came in, and now he's moving off. They only gave him five hundred for it, too."

Mr. Donovan turned a corner just then and came to a stop beside his well. There were a great many cars parked beside the derrick—so many, in fact, and so many people standing in the way, that Miss Carrie could see very little until Mr. Donovan had helped her up the oil-spattered steps to the derrick floor. Even then she saw little enough that she could understand. There was a greasy contrivance, with many wheels, which Mr. Donovan called a Christmas tree; and a pool of mud spread over with swirls of purple oil, which he called a slushpit; and a great deal of machinery, and a pipe running down to a row of tanks; and another pipe running over to three great boilers, whose stacks were wired to trees; and a tall iron mast which was hissing and spraying a mist of black oil on the corner of a cabin.

So this was an oil well!

And this was the Negro's cabin!

It was a cabin, she could see, like any other in the piney woods—a two-room shelter, with a sagging gallery, a homemade mud chimney, a plank outside the door for the washbasin, collards blooming yellow in the garden patch, a gate made from part of a bedstead . . .

When Mr. Donovan went off, presently, to inspect his tanks, she walked over to it. Around the corner behind the cabin, the Negro was moving out. He had loaded his wife and his children and his dog and his chickens and his hogs into a ramshackle wagon, along with the washtubs and mattresses and quilts; he had fastened the bedsprings to the side; now he was trying to back a stubborn mule between the shafts. Where would they go? she wondered. Where would they find a home?

She walked back to Mr. Donovan's car and smoothed the newspaper under her as she sat down. She was very tired, and the smell of gas and oil had made her a little sick. Resting her head in the corner, she closed her eyes and clasped her gloves in her lap. It would have been better, she told herself, if she had stayed at home this morning. The well had been so little to see; and the old Negro moving out—that troubled her. It made her wonder if sooner or later, they would not all of them be turned out of their homes—if they were not all of them, like Esau of old, selling their birthright for a mess of pottage.

The following is a biographical sketch of the author's paternal grand-mother. Not originally intended for publication, it was written by Winifred Sanford for her family in the 1950s.

A Victorian Grandmother

She was never one to store away keepsakes of her past, nor, for that matter, to imagine that anything concerning her might be of interest to her children. Although she lived to be ninety-seven years old (she was ten years old when Victoria took her throne, and lived more than twenty years after Victoria was dead), she was seldom known to indulge in reminiscence, but was always a little apologetic when she recalled some happenings of long ago in Ireland. She did not consider her own life of any particular importance.

So it happened that I, her granddaughter, was grown before I saw the only picture of her youth of which I have any knowledge. It is not dated, but must have been taken when she was not more than twenty, for there is a certain grace and dreaminess which stiffened as she grew older. When she was very old, an amateur palmist once read her hand. "I see an early love affair," she ventured, "with an unhappy ending."

"That is indeed true," said my grandmother, as though she were speaking of someone else. "I was once engaged to marry an officer in the army, who died of a fever." None of us had ever heard of him before. For all I know this picture may have been taken for him, but then, of course, it may not.

At any rate she sits with hands tightly joined in her lap, and her parted hair falling in ringlets over her ears—very sweet, but a little prim, in her stiff taffeta frock with its white embroidered collar and cuffs. Even then, I observe, embroidery! It was a passion which has always seemed one of the delightful inconsistencies of her character. Embroidery seems so frivolous an occupation for so strong-minded a woman—mere punching of holes and drawing through the thread; yet for the last twenty years of her life, at least, she did little else. What dozens of shirtwaists, what hundreds of tablecloths and napkins she embroidered!

Yet here, as elsewhere, she was not altogether docile. She had her principles. She would, for instance, work no silly butterflies or birds—nothing, if you please, but flowers and leaves and scrolls. Only white on white, she contended, looked really well. And for coarse work, for anything heavy and quick and bold, she had the greatest contempt. She would condescend to try it if she had to—if it were a choice between that and sitting idle, but she did it unwillingly and in the spirit of sacrifice. Nor would she, when she was old, at least, wear a single stitch of embroidery herself. That is why her girlhood picture gave me such a start of surprise.

It was characteristic of her that as her magnificent eyesight failed at last, and her fingers became crippled with rheumatism, she continued to embroider unperturbed. "This will do well enough," she would say. If anything was wrong it was the vision of others; her own standards she never doubted.

This, I believe, was her dominant trait. She was a rock upon which others were dashed to spray. In a world turned upside down in her lifetime by science and psychology and machinery, she was unmoved. Not, however, through egotism. Quite the contrary. It was obedience, rather. She believed, as a matter of course—nay— as a matter of duty, what she had been taught as a girl in Ireland in the second quarter of the nineteenth century.

She knew, absolutely, right from wrong. There was simply no arguing with her. She clung, for instance, to certain eighteenth-century pronunciations, in spite of the dictionaries, relying with splendid obstinacy upon her father's word. She would not condescend to eat tomatoes because her father had not regarded them as food. Love apples, he called them, and grew them like flowers in his garden. In larger matters she was quite as obdurate. She, who had seen the great Irish famine, had learned once for all time that extravagance was wrong and that thrift, no matter how extreme or unnecessary, was right. She spoke once of a dress which she wore when Grandfather was courting her, the skirt of which had been torn and neatly darned. The sight of this thriftiness, and perhaps her own lack of self-consciousness, moved Grandfather to make a request. Would she, he asked, be willing to wear the same garment on their wedding journey? She would and she did and she was proud of it.

To the extravagance of young America she was never able to reconcile herself. All this money spent for nonsense! When it could have been put away for posterity! She could never understand that conditions were altogether different from those she had known in her youth in a poor land, where inheritance counted for everything, and where money could not be made, and must, therefore, be saved. I remember how she once denounced a young girl of our acquaintance for buying new furs, when there were people without food enough to keep them alive.

For herself, she spent, as nearly as possible, nothing. I remember her seventieth birthday. "I do not expect to outlive the year," she announced with no sign of regret or dismay. "All my relatives have died at the age of seventy." And since she would not live through the year, she would buy no new clothes. The old ones would do well enough. Who could guess that she had more than a quarter of her life still before her, in the course of which she never made a purchase except under protest? Even then she insisted on the cheapest and least stylish garment procurable. Smile, if you like, at the picture of my grandmother, with her widow's veil framing her face, and her folded hands disdaining to lift her skirt, demanding of a twentieth-century saleswoman a coat "which is quite out of style." She would have felt silly and frivolous in anything else.

Although she considered money of the greatest importance, she could never understand the credit system or the most elementary working of a bank. A dollar to her was an actual dollar and she never quite believed that checks were worth the paper upon which they were written. If one of her sons insisted on having her signature on the dotted line, she signed, though reluctantly. It seemed to her suspiciously like nonsense. When she made gifts, as always on Christmas and birthdays, and often for no reason at all except the compulsion of her affection, she sent the actual currency, nobly indifferent to the hazards of the postal system. She would not have felt that she had sent anything at all if she had sent a check.

Her sons, too, had the greatest difficulty in persuading her to deposit her money in the bank. She much preferred to carry it in a bulging wad, in that mysterious pocket she had retained in her petticoat through all the changes of fashion, and from which, with her magnificent dignity, which nothing ever ruffled, she would draw it forth when the occasion demanded. That curious people might be staring at her in public places, that they might think her ridiculous as she lifted her outer skirt and delved into the pocket of her petticoat, never occurred to her. If it had, she would not have been dismayed. Her money was safe, and she was carrying it where she had been taught to carry it as a girl. What more was there to be said?

Although there is a family tradition that she was the first woman to take out naturalization papers (I have never been able to verify this), she was never in the least Americanized. And she did not want to be. She never quite trusted this new country where the standards she knew to be right were so often reversed or ignored. In the last year of her life, when a long illness had somewhat affected her mind, she was heard to refer to "whoever passes for the government in this country." She was prejudiced, I suppose, from the first. Had she not seen my grandfather convert all his possessions in Ireland into cash, which he packed in a trunk for the journey, lest he be cheated by the banks? Had she not walked the pavements of New York seeking a hotel where the meats were roasted on a spit, as at home? Had not a young lady in a house where they stayed gone into ecstasies about a very inferior ballad called "Dixie," which Grandmother had been kind enough to pick out for her on the piano, but which had no musical merit whatever? Was not the whole country for which she had left everything that was dear to her in the past— the River Shannon, where her brothers used to fish, the Lakes of Killarney, where she went, in her mended dress, on her wedding trip, the Vale of Avoca, where the three rivers met near the cottage where she had lived after her marriage, the patch of woodland through which she had seen my grandfather, for the first time, hunting with his hounds—was not the country for which she had left all this engaged in a foolish civil war of which she could make neither head nor tail? Wasn't everything, I can imagine her asking herself as she went serenely about her own affairs, in her own way, wasn't everything topsy-turvy?

So I think she laid all the startling changes that took place in her long life to the account of America. It was here that she saw women leaving their homes for silly clubs and sillier offices. It was here that her grandchildren grew up, talking like barbarians and ignorant of French. It was here that she saw the landscape strung with telegraph and telephone wires. I am not sure that she was ever able to bring herself to talk over a telephone. "Mark my word," I remember her saying. "No good will come of this." She made up her mind that the end of the world would come through some gigantic short circuit. It was all foolishness. Even plumbing and electric lighting seemed to compromise her a little with her archenemy—luxury. The only innovation she really enjoyed was the automobile, and she was apologetic about that. It seemed, really, too easy a way to get around.

Above all, she regretted the lack of discipline. In her day, children were taught obedience, and wives, acquiescence. Opinionated though she was, she never, so far as I know, failed to defer to her husband. She had been too carefully trained in the Victorian tradition for that. It was the duty of a wife to be self-effacing. If my grandfather spent an inordinate amount of money for books, she did not protest. If he wrote about history, about religion, about science—for he was interested in everything—I am sure she never reproved him. Even when he invested his capital in mining stocks, and insisted on visiting the mines in person and assaying the ores himself, she kept silence. If things went wrong, and dividends failed to arrive, it was due, of course, to the extravagance and foolishness of America. "I do not know what is to become of this country," she would say, sadly.

One change, however, she could not altogether ignore, and that was age. She found it humiliating. She was a woman of unusual vigor, who had never in her whole life been so tired that a fifteen-minute rest would not revive her, and it annoyed her to be treated as feeble. She could not bear to have us run upstairs for her glasses. When she traveled, she would angrily insist on carrying her own bags. She was insulted when anyone offered her a seat on a streetcar. And I remember an almost violent argument about a Pullman berth, which seemed to her utter nonsense. She must have been well past eighty at the time, and she wanted to sit up all night in the day coach.

Yet, in her armor of self-discipline, there were little flaws of grace and sentiment. She was strict with children, and I can still hear her stern voice saying, "Do not meddle!" But with babies she was charming. She would trot them on her knee and actually talk baby talk and make faces for their amusement. With all her parsimony—and it was irritating at times—she was generous with her children and grandchildren. If they needed money, they should have it. She had given away, long before she died, every personal relic of the past, so that she hadn't a single jewel, a single book except her Bible and a volume called *Daily Bread*, or a keepsake except her family photographs. The Christmas presents of one year were usually given away before the next. What use did she have for fine leather traveling bags? Or bathrobes? Or fancy quilts? She was always upset at Christmastime because, in spite of her warnings, people would give her presents which she was too honest to say she enjoyed.

About unimportant things she was amusingly positive. Girls, for instance, should have small mouths. Large mouths she abhorred. Indeed for so practical a person she had a surprising insistence on beauty. Tea, for another thing, should be made of a certain strength. Yet this was in direct contradiction to her other maxims about food. She went on the theory that it was all nonsense to be critical of food. One should eat what was placed before him, and one should consume all of it, as she had been taught in her girlhood, even to his glass of water. But with tea—and with toast—she was fond of both— she found the case a little different. Tea that was too weak was insipid, tea that was too strong was injurious, and toast, of course, should be brown—burned, if need be, but never pale. She was extremely particular about both, and she explained away the contradiction with her usual logic; those who liked tea or toast otherwise were simply being fussy.

She was the last person in the world, of course, to preach any sort of cant. Knowing right from wrong as she did, she was not averse to passing judgment, but it was never with any thought of self-righteousness or any sentimentality. The insipid or sugary in religion disgusted her. And yet, matter-of-fact as she was, plainspoken and frugal with verbal embroidery, she had her emotions, which were for that reason, perhaps, the deeper. When the occasion demanded it, she was not ashamed of tears. And she had, for all her scorn of individuals, an immense pity for life. I never think of her now without remembering one night, when I walked upstairs with her as a small child. She gave me no caress, but climbed ahead of me in her stately manner until she reached the stair landing from which a window looked out over the city. There she paused a moment. The wind was whistling about the house, shaking the windowpanes and bending the trees in the yard below. Far away were the small cold lights of the city; farther still, the bright beam of the lighthouse on the harbor pier. "The foxes have holes," quoted my grandmother, suddenly, "and the birds of the air have nests, but the Son of Man hath nowhere to lay His head." She made no further comment, and after a minute she went on upstairs, walking slowly, as always, with her usual calm dignity.

Afterword

British writer Virginia Woolf suggested in 1929 that women who create fiction may be compelled to write "shorter, more concentrated" works since they will rarely have the time for lengthy research and can always expect to be interrupted. "For interruptions there will always be," she adds. Novelist Woolf, who in her plea for "a room of one's own" expresses the woman writer's longing for time and solitude in which to create, seems to have had novelists in mind when she warned of the inevitable intrusion of other responsibilities upon women who long to write on a regular schedule. In the decade that Woolf voiced her perceptions of the writing woman's dilemma, several Texas women were already exploring shorter forms for their fiction. The genre that they chose for presenting their narratives, however, was not that of an abbreviated novel but the short story form.

In 1925 Edward J. O'Brien, editor of the long-lived Best Short Stories series, praised the form as uniquely suited to self-expression for both men and women writers of America. Traditional fictional forms all too often echoed European values, he said. The next year O'Brien selected Winifred Sanford's short story "Windfall" as one of the best. Women writers of the 1920s who chose to write short stories, however, probably did so neither because of limited writing time nor out of nationalistic pride in developing a form that Americans could call their own. Very likely their strongest motivation for writing short fiction was its marketability. Both popular magazines

173

and literary journals of the day were publishing several short stories each issue, offering considerable opportunity for writers of short fiction. Three of Winifred Sanford's short stories were published in *Woman's Home Companion*. Significantly, nine others appeared in *The American Mercury*, edited by H. L. Mencken, who, as Sanford's daughter remembers in the foreword to this volume, "was constantly exhorting her to send more material." *The American Mercury*, under Mencken's guidance from its founding in 1924 until his retirement in 1933, also published the likes of Lewis Mumford, Sinclair Lewis, Carl Sandburg, and Vachel Lindsay. That Mencken found Sanford's stories as worthy of publication as the works of these highly regarded writers validates a conjecture that had she continued to create fiction, Sanford might have received recognition beyond that of readers of *The American Mercury* and anthologists of Texas fiction.

Mencken begins his *In Defense of Women* (1918; revised in 1922) with an analysis of the feminine mind in which he declares that women "are the supreme realists of the race." They are so, he proclaims, because of their singular talent for separating the appearance from the substance. He concludes, "They see at a glance what most men could not see with searchlights and telescopes; they are at grips with the essentials of a problem before men have finished debating the mere externals." Whatever rebuttals Mencken's opinions may stir in the reader, it seems clear in what he says here why he admired Winifred Sanford's fiction. She writes with the confidence of one who understands the conflicts in the human spirit which motivate the actions of men and women. Appearance and substance alike are important to her art.

Winifred Sanford came to Texas in 1920 with her young attorney husband. The booming oil fields around Wichita Falls gave her husband the opportunity to establish a practice in oil and gas law and provided Sanford with the material for one of her best-known stories, "Windfall," as well as several others. Fourteen years after the couple left Wichita Falls for the East Texas oil fields, San-

ford wrote with regret to fiction writer and editor Margaret Cousins
that she missed the stimulation of meeting with members of the
Manuscript Club, a writers' group she had helped to found soon
after her arrival in Wichita Falls. Once she left that supportive
group, Sanford felt cut off from inspiration. What she is not likely to
have known is that through her writing she had become part of a
Texas woman's literary tradition initiated in 1833 by Stephen F. Austin's cousin Mary Austin Holley, who published her first account of
Texas colonial life and times that year. Among Texas women of the
nineteenth century who also succeeded as writers were Amelia Barr
and Mollie E. Moore Davis. Widowed shortly after the Civil War
by a yellow fever epidemic, Barr supported her surviving daughters
by writing historical novels. Davis, despite her busy life as wife of a
newspaperman, published two popular novels, *Under the Man-Fig*
(1895) and *The Wire Cutters* (1899), before the turn of the century.
Knowing that heritage and the successes as well as the failures of the
women writers who stayed with the writing life during the nineteenth and early twentieth centuries might have encouraged Winifred Sanford to continue developing her talents.

In 1936 Sanford took advantage of the opportunity to unite
with other Texas writers in a statewide effort to identify and gather
into one supportive organization those associated with developing
the literary tradition of the state. Her name appears on the original
roster of the Texas Institute of Letters with those of Karle Wilson
Baker, poet and novelist from Nacogdoches, and Rebecca Smith,
who would co-author (with Mabel Major and T. M. Pearce) the first
edition of *Southwest Heritage*, a literary history of Texas writing
published in 1938. Men of letters, however, seemed to dominate the
first two sessions. J. Frank Dobie spoke at the first meeting, admon-
ishing charter members of TIL to value their heritage but to explore
new forms, particularly the novel.

Women writers contributed noticeably to the success of the
third session in 1938, however. Karle Wilson Baker was elected
president, and Laura Krey, whose historical novel *And Tell of Time*

had just been published and was destined to become a bestseller, spoke to an overflow crowd on Friday evening. Winifred Sanford also participated that year in a symposium on fiction conducted by Baker. William Vann's history of TIL does not speak again of Winifred Sanford's contributions to the organization, but her activities with TIL in the mid- and late 1930s suggest that Sanford, by now the mother of three, must have expected to resume her writing career for several years after the publication of her last story in 1931.

Membership in a writers' organization that met only once a year was not enough, however, to sustain that "old competitive spirit," which inspired one to write "in spite of yourself." Winifred Sanford's story is not much different from that of her contemporaries among women writers. Although most continued writing for thirty years or so, only a few produced more than two or three novels or a dozen or so published stories. One exception, Norma Patterson, more prolific than most Texas women of that time, published more than two hundred short stories in the *Saturday Evening Post* and other magazines and a dozen popular novels as well. Sanford's correspondent Margaret Cousins, a native Texan, also was a successful author of periodical fiction. But Katherine Anne Porter, who began establishing her reputation in the 1920s, produced a body of work which takes up scarcely a scant foot on the bookshelf. Karle Wilson Baker published several volumes of poetry but only two novels. Ruth Cross published two novels and Dorothy Scarborough five, but each is remembered for only one work. Cross's *The Golden Cocoon* appeared in 1924; *The Wind*, Scarborough's controversial portrayal of women's lives on the Texas frontier, appeared the following year.

It is certain that most of the women writers who were publishing at the time that Winifred Sanford's stories appeared struggled to structure a compromise in roles so that they could both manage a home and create fiction. As with Winifred Sanford, they seldom discovered a quiet place of their own. However, although their limited creative hours may have curtailed their production, as this slender collection of Winifred Sanford's work demonstrates, these writers seldom aimed for quantity. Their purpose as writers seems to have been twofold. They longed to examine experience and see in "the meaning of all this," as Virginia Woolf describes the writer's vision, truths that would inform the spirits of those who chose to read their stories. As Katherine Anne Porter's polished narratives exemplify, they worked hard, too, at perfecting their craft of storytelling.

Winifred Sanford wrestled, often successfully, with both challenges. Her classic work "Windfall" is the story of an inarticulate farm woman whose intuitive uneasiness tells her that her family's values will be altered negatively and permanently by the sudden bonanza of oil production on their hardscrabble farm. The trespassing crowds from town, who trample their cotton and cut tracks across their pastures in their eagerness to see the site where black gold flows out of the ground, represent to Cora the destruction of life as she has known it. Cora could not say it that way, but her thoughts and responses on that hot day when she first sees oil reveal the turmoil in her spirit.

"Windfall" appeared in *The American Mercury* in June of 1928, making Winifred Sanford the first Southwestern author to examine fictionally the alternate joy and despair that the discovery of oil on Texas land could precipitate in human lives. It was almost ten years later that Karle Wilson Baker's novel *Family Style* (1938) on the same theme appeared. In 1941 Mary King wrote of a Texas boomtown from an adolescent girl's point of view in *Quince Bolivar*. Jewel Gibson's *Black Gold* (1950) continued the tradition. William A. Owens was one of the first male Texas writers to treat the subject fictionally in *Fever in the Earth*, published in 1958. Of these works, only Owens's novel and Sanford's story have continued to be reprinted. Hilton Ross Greer included "Windfall" in his 1928 collection *Best Short Stories of the Southwest*, which also contains stories by Dorothy Scarborough, Mary Austin, and Norma Patterson. Greer praises his selections for their "impressive characterizations and . . . stark realism that go to the heart of life as life is anywhere. . . ."

Two years later the story appeared in an English composition text-book as a model for developing writers, and again in 1954 in the popular anthology *21 Texas Short Stories*, edited by William Peery and reprinted several times since its first edition. In his biographical introduction to Sanford's story, Peery calls the story an "excellent study of the effect of newly discovered Texas oil on the life of a simple farm woman." He adds that the story will "remain some-thing of a classic in the literature of the oil fields."

With equal insight into the personalities of oil well promoter and oil rig roughneck, Sanford writes as convincingly from the male point of view as the woman's in her three other narratives of early boom days activities. In "Luck" she reveals her remarkable knowl-edge of the operation of the early rotary rig, the dangers involved in pulling drill pipe and drilling in inclement weather, and the certain tragic consequences of an uncontrolled oil well blowout. The bitter, ironic conclusion reenacts the hundreds of derrick accidents occur-ring in every new field where desperate promoters down on their luck gambled that the next one would turn their fortunes around. The riches-to-rags theme of "Mr. Carmichael's Room," which also has been anthologized, and the return to the concerns of "Wind-fall" in "Fever in the South" complete the writer's exploration of fre-netic oil boom life. In "Fever in the South," she writes once again of the displacement of those whom fate has placed in the way of the promoter hunting more land that he hopes to convince investors lies over black gold. In these four stories Sanford portrays comprehen-sively the greed, the excitement, and the inevitable tragedies of life in the oil boom towns of the 1920s.

Winifred Sanford's astute examination of fundamentalist reli-gion and the lives of Southern blacks in "Saved" and "Black Child" exemplifies her versatility as well as her sensitive response to the life surrounding her after she settled in Texas. Her memories of Minne-sota life remained keen as well, as she proves in "The Blue Spruce." Snow imagery intensifies the irony in her description of a skiing duel between two hulking Scandinavians intimidated by a "little blue spruce." Stylistically, this is one of the writer's better narratives.

Winifred Sanford's subjects vary widely, but she has missed little in her perceptive observation of human experience. More important than her realistic portrayal of observable life, however, is her sure knowledge of interior life—of human motivations and self-delusions. We may regret that Winifred Sanford wrote so little. Better still, we can be grateful that she is one of those writers of the 1920s who gained for Texas authors the attention of both critics and readers and put them on the alert that women's fiction had moved into the mainstream of the state's growing literary tradition. They provided the impetus for further development of fictional forms by women writers and showed those who followed that the woman writer can produce quality work even when its quantity is limited by life's circumstances.

Lou Halsell Rodenberger
McMurry College